MURDER IN THE SKIES

A RITCHIE AND FITZ SCI-FI MURDER MYSTERY

KATE MACLEOD

1

EVERY TIME MURDINA RITCHIE set foot in the hangar of the Oymyakon Foreign Service Academy, she felt just as overwhelmed—as awe-struck—as she had the very first time she had seen it.

It wasn't because it was a cavernously large space. Granted, growing up in an overcrowded space station made her far more accustomed to small spaces, but still. She had been inside big, open structures before. Open space didn't bother her.

On the other hand, it wasn't the fact that this hangar was closed off from the sky that bothered her, either. She knew the sky was just a short journey up one of the many aircraft elevators, and there was nothing more than a door between her and that openness. Those doors kept the wind out, and after her first semester at the academy, she'd seen enough storms to know why keeping equipment out of that wind was important.

Wind was a new thing for her, but she found it quite exhilarating, even when it was bone-chillingly cold and carrying droplets of rain that stung when they struck her face.

No, what was overwhelming about the hangar was its location in the heart of the mountain. It was hard to put it out of her mind, the thought of all of that stone overhead, just waiting to crush all of this like so many toys. And her with it.

She had gotten used to tuning out that feeling while in the dormitories, which were technically deeper within the mountain than the hangar. But the walls there were lined with panels, the floors and ceilings covered with tile. It was easy to imagine she was back home on the space station, where the thought of the vacuum of space all around her with all of its dangers had never once entered her mind.

But here in the hangar, the floors were bare stone, the walls were bare stone, the ceilings were bare stone. There was no way *not* to know she was standing inside a mountain.

And maybe that mountain didn't want her there.

She had only been in the hangar a few times that first semester. Before she could go up in a glider, she had to complete all the ground school work the rest of her classmates had done the year before. She had worked hard, but it had still been nearly the end of the semester before she had passed that test and had been allowed to sit behind the controls.

When the second semester started, she would be crossing this hangar three times a week, every week. For the rest of this year and for every year after that she remained at the academy. She had to get used to it.

Not that she had told Colonel Hansen about her struggle to control her fear when she had asked for permission to get flight hours in over the inter-semester break. No, officially, she was getting more practice time in because the few flights she had done after passing ground school had been very rough. She needed extra time to build up her basic skills.

Which was totally true, but she worried about that less. Having to work harder, to prove herself worthy of being here? That she was used to. She had no problem with that.

But the thought of all the stone over her head, waiting to smash her like a bug?

"Ugh," Ritchie said, speeding her steps until her glider came into view. It was a gorgeous thing, even here in the murky dark. The other cadets hated these gliders. Being a remote and underfunded school, the Oymyakon Foreign Service Academy had the worst examples of everything, and that included these outdated gliders. But to Ritchie's eyes, it wasn't so much old as classic, from back when designers still wanted things to have a certain beauty to their form.

Plus, it was gold. Well, sickly yellowish-green under the hangar lights. But in the sunlight? Pure gold.

Ritchie climbed into the cockpit, buckling in before putting on her helmet. It adjusted to fit optimally around her skull as if it were built just for her, but the odor from the last cadet who had been assigned that helmet still lingered. Fear sweat.

"Cadet?" Colonel Hansen's voice came in over the comm. Physically, he was in the command room on the end of the hangar deck, but the screens there gave him views of everything on the deck and in the sky.

"Running preflight checklist now," she said. The glider had very few systems, so this was a short task. "How's the weather?"

"Iffy," he said, which in her experience was usually how the weather was on Oymyakon. "Nothing you can't handle."

"Yes, sir," Ritchie said. "I'm good to go."

"The lift is on its way to you now," Hansen said. She turned in the cockpit to see the square of metal skimming over the stone hangar floor. It slipped under her glider with only a small jostling when it passed itself under the wheels of her landing gear.

Then she was moving backward, away from the cavern wall and towards the center of the cavernous space. The quality of the light around her changed slightly, and she knew the door at the top of the shaft over her was open now, but that the skies above were too dark to illuminate anything below.

As her glider moved up, the hangar passed out of sight. Nothing to see now but more rough-hewn stone much closer outside the cockpit windows. Ritchie checked her seat restraints, then the strap on her helmet, then ran down the same preflight checklist another time.

Then her glider was out in the wind, and that oppressive feeling of being trapped under stone finally passed. The wings rocked gently at the buffets of air. The wind couldn't do more to her glider than that even when the whistle built up to a shriek as it whipped past her cockpit; the lift platform was still holding her glider firmly as it carried her to the first of a long row of launching stations.

She came to a halt sitting at a steep angle, her back pressed against the seat behind her.

"Launching in five," Hansen said.

"Roger," Ritchie said and pulled down her helmet's visor. Its holographic display surrounded her, measuring the distance between her and the most prominent of the clouds above her, between her and the mountain peak off to her left, between her and tip of the launch station just visible in front of her glider's nose.

She focused her gaze directly in front of her and ignored the toggling numbers as one billow of cloud or another moved to the fore. Hansen was still counting down in her ear. She just had time to take one last deep breath.

Then the launch system fired her glider up into the air. She kept her hands off the controls as she was pressed even deeper into the seat behind her. A metallic taste spread over her tongue, and she realized too late that she had once more been nervously chewing at her lip and had bitten down hard at the moment of launch.

Bad habit.

She punched through layer after layer of clouds, water droplets striking the cockpit window only to be streaked away.

Then she was through, past the highest level of the storm, into clear, calm atmosphere. Her helmet visor immediately darkened the spot where the sun should be off to her right, preventing it from blinding her. The rest of the sky was a deep indigo blue, a color of sky she never saw down on the ground, even when the clouds briefly parted.

If she kept going, she'd be in space. She was so close.

But without a source of propulsion, her glider couldn't keep going. Its ascent was slowing down, coming to an end.

Ritchie put her hands on the controls, leveling out before she had quite lost the last of her momentum. Then she started scanning the skies around her.

One minute she was alone in the sky; the next, she was surrounded by enemy fighters.

She knew they were figments, that if she lifted her visor with its holographic display, she would see nothing but the tops of the clouds and all of that indigo sky, but with her visor down, they looked so real. The one directly in front of her was so close she could hit it with a rock if she had one around to throw.

She could see sunlight dancing over its wings as it banked, the outline of helmet and flight suit of the pilot within, the movement as they raised a hand to flip a switch.

Then the glow deep within the barrel of its gun just before the laser fired.

Ritchie rolled her glider out of the way, then came around to fire herself.

Her first attempt at flying an actual glider had left her cursing the simulator back home she had thought was teaching her all she needed to know. It had been even more inadequate than her scant knowledge of how to fly in atmosphere before she went through ground school here. But now, after days of flying morning, noon and night, it was like she could feel the patterns of the air around her. She could feel how to catch the pockets that would cradle her as if in the palm of some giant's hand and lift her back up into the sky.

It was like she could control that wind, to convince it to carry her glider around the sky. As exhilarating as the wind was down on the ground, it was far more so up in the sky.

Ritchie lost herself in the dance, staying out of the line of fire of all of those enemy ships but slipping in behind them to take them out one by one. It was almost relaxing.

But she couldn't stay up at that altitude forever. Soon the fight had sunk down into the clouds, the other fighters erupting from the storm around her with little warning, then losing her when she attempted to pursue them through the gray fog. When she shot one down, she could just hear the explosion, as if it were muffled by the fuselage around her and not just another part of the illusion.

Occasionally a rumble of thunder would rattle her glider. She could feel that rumble lingering in her chest, and from time to time she even thought she could smell ozone on the air. That was definitely not part of the simulation. The wind wanted to bounce her, to rip the yoke out of her hands, to throw her and the glider down to the ground below, but she had a feel for it now. She didn't fight it; she worked with it. She waited for every opportunity to turn that wind to her advantage, to get a clear shot at another enemy fighter.

Then she was through the bottom of the storm, the open fields that surrounded the school visible below, the grass flattening under bursts of wind. There were still a pair of fighters pursuing her. The wind around the mountains was even more chaotic than it was higher in the storm, but she was also more familiar with its vagaries. She took out the last two fighters, one after another, then pushed her visor back with a sharp exhale of breath.

It was the closest thing to a cheer she'd allow herself.

"Land on strip 45," Hansen said blandly in her ear.

"Roger," Ritchie said, then caught herself biting at her already sore lip again. Strip 45 always had a crazy crosswind. Ritchie was pretty sure it only existed to take advantage of that crazy crosswind for training purposes. She had wrecked her glider on four of her first five landings, much to everyone else's amusement.

And the weather that had been iffy when she had launched had downgraded significantly. But she could still feel the wind around her. It wasn't quite chaos. It would still hold her aloft if she let it.

She worked with it, moving the nose at an angle to the strip that would've freaked her out just a month ago. But she knew now to listen to the wind and not that panicking voice in her head.

She landed without a bounce, speeding down the strip until the landing system caught her.

Ritchie unbuckled from her seat and opened the cockpit, climbing out and dropping down to the ground still rolling beneath her. She hit the ground at a run parallel to the glider riding on its lift platform, then slowed to a walk and changed direction to meet Hansen walking towards her across the grassy field between the strip and the control tower where he had been supervising her flight.

He had his fur-lined cap pulled down low over his dark eyes and the collar of his jacket buttoned all the way up to his nose, but the scarf around his neck was dancing in the wind in a way that was eye-catching if not particularly functional. He never seemed particularly bothered by the cold, and Ritchie suspected he had been in much harsher environments during the military career that had eventually brought him to this remote world.

She still didn't know where he had gotten the scars that criss-crossed the olive skin of his face, deep furrows on one side tapering off to an almost beautiful filigree on the other. A particularly brutal environment was one theory among the cadets.

While she would still say that the bite of the wind was more reviving than any amount of coffee, she would also have to admit that on days like today when it made her eyes water, then froze that water to her lashes, it was a bit much.

The moment she and Hansen were within arm's reach of each other, they both turned to walk together towards the tall glassed facade of the academy's library building. The rest of the school was beyond that wall, tucked away inside the mountain. There was a warm familiarity with the way their strides just matched. But it was odd, that feeling of familiarity, because while Hansen had been the officer that escorted her to the academy, she had had no classes with him since and was only working with him now because most of the staff had left when the cadets did at the end of the last semester.

"How did it feel, cadet?" Hansen asked her first, as he always did.

"Pretty good," Ritchie said.

"It looked pretty good," he said. "You feel ready for the next semester?"

"I don't know," Ritchie said. "It's different when the other ships are actually around you, flown by other cadets." Cadets who were watching you. Judging you. But she didn't say that part out loud.

"Well, I'm not a combat flight instructor," Hansen said. "It's been years since I was in a glider, and I've never even actually flown combat myself. So I may not be the best judge of your skills. But I do think you're ready."

"Maybe I won't embarrass myself this time," she said.

"I think you're being too hard on yourself," he said.

"I won that simulation, sure, but barely," Ritchie said. "I had maybe another minute's worth of momentum going before I would've been a sitting duck, down on the ground where anyone could take me out."

"A win is a win," Hansen said. They were at the library steps now, carved out of the mountain's own stone in wide, shallow steps designed to encourage students to linger in groups or study there.

Not that anyone ever did. Whoever had designed it hadn't really understood about the wind and frequent cold rain, clearly.

The outer door opened as they approached, and they went inside, waiting in the entranceway as that door closed before the inside door opened. Hansen caught the end of his scarf, which was still whipping in the wind behind them, snatching it inside just before the door shut.

The sudden silence in that enclosed space was like a pressure on Ritchie's ears. But it only lasted a moment before the inner door hissed open.

"Ritchie," Hansen said before she could step away.

"Sir?" she said, but his attention appeared fixed on his own hands carefully folding the long scarf into a neat square. Only after he had tucked that square away in his inner coat pocket did he look up at her again.

"We agreed to try level five on that simulation, yes?" he said.

"Yes, sir," Ritchie said. That metallic taste was back, and she forced her teeth to let her lip go. Level five was beyond what the senior cadets were required to do, but she had wanted to push herself. Now she knew why she had succeeded, even if barely. Hansen had dialed it back without telling her.

"You just flew a level seven," he said. "And you did just fine. Don't worry about next week. Now, are you heading to the cafeteria?"

"No," Ritchie said, her head spinning at how fast he had just changed the subject. "I was going to study more before breaking for lunch."

"Study?" Hansen said, raising a single eyebrow.

"Current events, sir," Ritchie said. "I'm not behind the others in terms of diplomatic theory, but I'm missing a lot of cultural context in class discussions."

"Very good," Hansen said. "Do you mind checking in on Keller and Wyss? I see less of them than I do of you. Just remind them I'm available by comm if they need me."

"I will, sir," she said.

"Back to the grind tomorrow," Hansen said with what sounded like a sigh of regret. Then he gave her a little nod before heading across the open foyer at the heart of the library towards the main hall that led to the rest of the school, turning left to go down the administrative wing and disappearing from her sight.

Tomorrow. The rest of the cadets would be back from break tomorrow. She had lost track of the days. Her buddy Moreau would be back. Their roommates, Frei and Grof, would be back. She would once more fall asleep with the sounds of three other people softly breathing around her; that would be nice after days of that echoing emptiness broken only occasionally by the soft whir of a cleaning drone passing through.

Fitz would be back. Not that they had spent much time together over the last semester. He was new to this academy the same as she was, but he had transferred from another academy, a more respected one. He wasn't woefully behind the others like Ritchie was. Thankfully, Moreau was in the same boat with her in being new to the foreign service academy system, and they had supported each other through those first horrid weeks when all of their deficiencies came to light.

And with that thought, about those horrid weeks, she realized that Jeger also would be back, and all the good feelings that had coursed through her entire being at learning she had defeated a level seven simulation were gone in a flash.

Well, Jeger was always going to come back, Ritchie told herself, and went to find Keller and Wyss. Her steps were a bit more forceful than she intended, almost a stomping march. She stopped and took a deep breath.

There was nothing she could do about Jeger. She, along with Cadet Bale, were the two cadet captains, leaders of all the other students in the school. But where Cadet Bale liked to lead by example, putting himself in front of all the others and encouraging them to follow, Cadet Jeger had a more disciplinarian approach. She pushed those in the back to catch up with the others. Ritchie knew that she was in the back of her class in nearly every category, and she was working hard to catch up.

But no matter how Jeger framed her interactions with Ritchie,

Ritchie knew she wasn't really trying to help Ritchie succeed. On the contrary, she wanted her to fail. To drop out. To no longer be one of Jeger's problems.

What Ritchie couldn't ever figure out was if it was personal in any way. Had she done something to get on Jeger's bad side? Was there something she could do to change the way Jeger saw her?

She wished it was, but the more she searched for a reason, the less likely it seemed that there was one. It wasn't personal. She was just a number that Jeger didn't like. The last name on a list that needed to be shorter.

Ritchie took another deep breath, then resumed walking in a more normal stride. She had worked hard last semester to bring herself up to spec. Her instructors, while never effusive with their praise, had grudgingly accepted the results of her efforts. One way or another, Jeger was going to have to as well.

Ritchie crossed the foyer and turned into the library itself. Just being there went a long way towards quieting her mind. As much as she loved to fly, the library was her favorite place to be at the academy. Even in its current neat and tidy and echoingly empty state, it was a comfort. There was a reading nook set into the base of every tall window, with chairs drawn close together to catch whatever rare bit of sunlight might penetrate the cloud cover outside. The cushions in the reading chairs were fluffed up invitingly, spare readers resting on various little tables for cadets who had left theirs back in the barracks. The spine of the room was the single long table that looked like bare wood at the moment but was, in fact, a series of holographic workstations.

The space where the table stood was open all the way up to the ceiling four levels above, with the railings for balconies overlooking the table itself. Ritchie had not been up to those other levels since her first tour of the academy, but they held a variety of older model computers or computers that belonged to other species or cultures whose technology didn't interact neatly with that of the Union of Free Worlds. Some of the more advanced cadets with specific interests used them for specialized research.

But Ritchie's current destination was the glass-walled private conference rooms that stretched the length of the back wall. Each of these had its own holographic table with chairs around it. They were empty, gleamingly clean, with chairs arranged neatly around the central tables, ready for the rest of the cadets to return. All of them, that was, save for the very last room. She could hear voices coming from within, but the glass walls had been turned to opaque mode so that she couldn't see inside.

She raised a hand to knock, but then hesitated. She had been giving Wyss and especially Keller a wide berth since the other cadets had gone on vacation. Wyss was all right, but every conversation Ritchie had had with Keller had left her deeply bothered. The girl was forceful with her questions, oblivious to the feelings of others, and for someone with an interest in alien languages, shockingly unaware of social cues. She rubbed lots of cadets the wrong way, but she didn't seem to mind. Her ability to just not process other people's negative feelings towards her was kind of admirable in a way.

But she seemed to feel that Ritchie was her particular friend. And Ritchie had tried to be kind to her, at first, until it got just too exhausting. If Colonel Hansen hadn't specifically ordered her to do so, she'd never be going into this room and starting a conversation at all.

But he had ordered to do so. She just hoped that Keller didn't find some excuse to bring up Ritchie's father. Again.

Ritchie knocked briskly, then opened the door and stepped inside. Her eyes took a moment to adjust to the gloom within, but the assault of stale food odors and burnt coffee hit her at once.

"Hey, guys," Ritchie said, blinking until she could make out the silhouettes of their heads leaning close to the surface of the holographic tabletop. It wasn't set to projection mode, but the surface was covered with faint green sigils she couldn't make heads or tails of. "How's it going?"

"Abysmal," Keller said, waving a hand over the control to return the walls to full transparency, then dragging her hands through her thick red curls and leaving them more tangled than before. "We've been at this since the semester ended, and we have nothing to show for it. No progress at all."

Ritchie looked from Cadet Keller's freckled face to Wyss's pasty, pale one. Wyss just shrugged his shoulders.

"This is the written language of the cloud people of Grove Prime?" Ritchie asked. No one could pronounce what they called themselves, although computers could simulate it. Mainly because "cloud people" didn't mean people who lived in clouds or anything like that. It meant beings who were actual clouds. And yet were sentient. Naturally, their way of communicating was exceedingly *not* human.

Keller nodded. "Well, I'm not surprised. Advanced level linguists with multiple PhDs and years of experience haven't cracked this one. Did you really think you'd do it in fourteen days?"

Wyss gave a little laugh, but Keller flushed red. Clearly, she had expected just that. Then her face lit up. Ritchie felt a prickle of discomfort before Keller even spoke a word.

"But you recognized this as the manuscript of the cloud people," Keller said. "Is that because of your father's work with the gaseous species of the Vien District? Because a lot of people think they might be related."

"Keller," Wyss said softly, making a little negating gesture with his hand, but Keller ignored him.

"Your father made some significant breakthroughs in understanding how their written language differed from the spoken one," she went on. "I don't suppose you could find his notes for us on that? That would be *so* amazing. But anything you just remembered about it could help."

"I was five when he was working on that," Ritchie said. "I recognize the script, but not even from then. It's from my studies here." She put every bit of resistance to delve into this she could into her voice and her body language and hoped Keller would take the hint.

Usually, she didn't. She might not have this time either, but Wyss stepped in before she could speak.

"We're not giving up yet," Wyss said. "We're just out of ideas for how to tweak the algorithm. I know we're close, though. We just need some time away from the problem."

"And now we're going to get it whether we like it or not," Keller groused, flopping back into a chair and slouching down low.

"All of this training is important," Ritchie said, picking up a much-covered topic between them. "Even though you already know what you want to focus on, a wider education is valuable."

"Yeah, yeah," Keller said, still pouting. But then she perked up, sitting up in the chair to lean forward as she asked, "how did flight training go?"

"Well," Ritchie said. While a less delicate topic than her missing father, she didn't really want to discuss her academic problems with two novice cadets. They hadn't even started basic glider training yet.

"Your assessment or Hansen's?" Wyss asked, raising his eyebrows at that short answer.

"Both," Ritchie said.

"You'll show her," Keller said, nodding sagely. "She'll have to lighten up on you now."

Ritchie bit her lip, then flinched at the rawness of it, licking away another coppery splash of blood. She had to kick that habit, seriously.

Keller was still looking up at her with wide green eyes, waiting for Ritchie to say something.

To vent. That's what Keller wanted. Keller hated almost everything she was expected to do at the academy, and she wanted Ritchie to complain a little, too.

And the words were there, waiting to be spoken. Every frustration with Jeger and her unfair treatment of Ritchie. Of how hard Ritchie had worked, how much she deserved that work to be recognized. The words wanted to come out.

But not to Keller.

Not just because it would be bad for morale. Not because as a cadet of a higher class, she should set a better example for Keller, but also for Wyss, who was watching her closely as he waited to hear what she had to say.

No, in truth, it was because Keller wanted it too much. She had been trying to bond with Ritchie since the moment they met. Ritchie half suspected Keller was only here over break because she had known Ritchie would be, although how she had roped Wyss into also staying, she had no idea. Maybe their project really interested him that much; she didn't know.

But Ritchie was reluctant to be more than acquaintances with Keller. Not because they were in different years; Ritchie didn't really care about that, although many other cadets absolutely did. No, it was because constantly, when given any sort of opening at all, Keller wanted to grill Ritchie about her father, about his work, even about that last diplomatic assignment he had gone on. The one he hadn't come back from.

There was nothing Ritchie wanted to discuss less. But then, that was the whole reason for her even being in the library in the first place. She had to study up on current cultural and political situations because she had been purposefully tuning that out since the day her life went off the rails.

She could set her feelings aside to study things in an abstract way. She could block out the memories from her childhood of going over the current events with her diplomat father, who always asked for her take first before telling her his. Of the way he had treated her almost like an equal. At the very least, like her impressions were potentially something he could use in his own work.

Painful memories now. She could push them back while studying on her own, mostly.

But Keller pushed for more. She insisted on dredging them all up.

Not maliciously. Ritchie understood why Keller kept asking about things her father had said or wrote, or what he had said to her when she was still a girl. Keller had a fascination with how very alien species communicated with humans and how humans could better communicate with them. That had been her father's focus as well. And he had been very good at it.

Until the day it all went wrong. Until that last diplomatic summit with the Yuffids had seemed to be going swimmingly right up to that last minute when her father was beaten unconscious in front of the cameras streaming it all over the Union of Free Worlds. And no one knew for sure if he even still lived. The Yuffids had refused to speak to any human since.

"It will be fine," Ritchie said, not sure if she meant her problems with Jeger, or their struggles with the translation algorithm, or her own shattered childhood. Maybe all at once. "Colonel Hansen says to message him if you need anything."

Then she left the room, burying her hands deep in her flight suit pockets, all thoughts of studying gone now.

She needed more people around her. She wasn't exactly popular, but the crush of other cadets was a comfort.

She was glad the break was nearly over, even if it would mean dealing with Jeger again on a daily basis.

2

SHACKLETON FITZ IV stood at the shuttle window, bobbing his head to the driving beat of the music that filled the lounge and shuffling forkfuls of beef and broccoli noodle bowl into his mouth.

He wasn't going to get luxury like this when he disembarked at the Oymyakon Foreign Service Academy. Gone would be the chairs covered in leather as warm and soft as butter that molded to his form when he sat on them. Gone would be the music playing out loud and filling the space around him, not just through his implant for his ears only. Gone would be access to his own replicator that already knew all of his favorite dishes.

Gone would be beef and broccoli noodle bowls. The academy mess hall wasn't bad, but it wasn't great either.

Still, even with everything his father's private shuttle could offer him, he wished he was going back on the intergalactic railway again. He had been hoping to see the VIP car steward again, Tassa Sokolov. He had never gotten a chance to say a proper goodbye, and she hadn't been on the crew on his trip out.

If she didn't work for the railway anymore, he hoped it was because she had moved up in the universe. She was an excellent steward, but she could be an even more excellent... well, just about anything else. Her fast thinking had saved his friend Murdina Ritchie. And he hated that he'd missed his chance to thank her for that.

The aft door opened with a hiss, and without any command from anybody, the music instantly dropped to a volume little more than a hum.

"Stop playback," Fitz said with a sigh. The music he liked wasn't suited to soft background noise.

The system was programmed to lower the volume when either of his parents entered the room, but he didn't need to turn around to know it was his mother coming in to see him.

"Hey, mom," he said before shoving another forkful of food into his mouth. In case he needed a reason not to answer whatever she was about to say.

Fitz was standing with his backside resting against the back of one of the seats, timing his bites around the rocking of the shuttle around him. Now they hit a pocket of turbulence that made it feel like the entire shuttle floor was dropping out beneath them, then rushing back up and shaking like a horse trying to dislodge its rider. Fitz left the fork in his mouth, putting a hand on the fuselage to brace himself. He stayed on his feet, just barely.

But as much as his mother might be retired from the world of dance, she still moved with all the grace she had had in her heyday. She didn't even reach out to touch the seatbacks around her, just rode the wave as if she had long rehearsed every movement the shuttle was about to execute around her. Her short, bouncy hair rose up and dropped back down, and the fluttering back of her long sweater matched it, but her feet never faltered.

"Shack, take that fork out of your mouth," she said. Her tone was mock-stern, but he knew behind it was real concern. He sucked the sauce off the tines, then pulled it out.

"Sorry," he said. "I suppose you're going to tell me I could stab my brain?"

"I was going to tell you to buckle in," she said, grabbing his shoulder to turn him around, then push him back into the waiting seat. Not that she could move him around if he didn't choose to let her; she was half his size. But he slumped into the chair and let the chair extend restraints around him.

"The railway ride was smoother," Fitz said as his mother sat down beside him and snuggled back into the cushioned seat as the chair wrapped the restraints around her as well.

"Oh, I doubt that's true," she said. "Your father is an excellent pilot."

"A-ha," Fitz said, pronouncing each syllable distinctly.

"You know he is, Shack," his mother said chidingly. "He's circling again to see if there's a better opening in the storm, but it's looking pretty rough down there."

"It always is," Fitz said. "He's not going to find anything better. There's a reason Oymyakon is barely populated. And it's not just because it's light-years from anywhere."

"I'd be careful how you express your opinions about the place," she said. "We all know why you ended up here."

"Yeah," Fitz said, stirring at the remaining noodles before setting the bowl aside. He was no longer hungry.

"Shack," his mother said cajolingly.

"Please don't," he said. "There's nothing more to say. Father was perfectly clear."

"He was just angry," she said.

"He's always angry."

"No, he isn't."

"Well, he is with me."

"No, he isn't," she said more firmly. "He just wants to see you do well. We all know you're capable enough to succeed at anything. You just have to choose to do so."

"Yeah, just choose," Fitz said, turning away from her to look out the window at the grayish-black planet below. What kind of planet was black? Planets were supposed to be where you went for real sunshine, maybe a nice gleaming ocean or two.

"The only thing that's been holding you back is you," she said. "You know this is true."

"Maybe," Fitz said. "But it doesn't matter, does it? There's pretty much no point in even taking me back to the academy. He already thinks I've failed."

"That's not true," she said, but when he turned to give her a pointed look, she dropped her eyes. "Okay, it's a little bit true. But you have the power to make it not absolutely true."

"I have the power to not get kicked out of this last foreign service academy," Fitz said. "Maybe," he amended. "But I don't have the power to change how he perceives me. Nope. That's impossible."

"If you succeed, he will see it."

"I doubt it," Fitz said, but only to himself under his breath after he'd turned back to the window. They were descending into the storm, droplets of water streaking across the window in ever-thickening streams.

"I know you didn't mean it when you said you were going to go AWOL from the academy," she said.

"Really? Because I kind of thought I meant it."

"No, you didn't," she said.

"But he meant what he said," Fitz said, poking a finger in the general direction of the shuttle cockpit. "If I scrub out of this academy, he'll drop me off at the nearest enlistment station, and I can work my way up from the bottom like he did." By the end of that sentence, his words were dripping with disdain. "But did he, though? Work his way up from the bottom with no help from others?"

"It doesn't matter," his mother said. "It was an empty threat. It will never happen because you're not going to get another disciplinary mark against you. Right?"

"He meant it."

"In the moment, maybe," she conceded. "But his anger cools, you know it does."

"He still means it now," Fitz said. "If I get kicked out of this academy, you're both done with me. I'm on my own. I can join the general infantry, or I can make my own way through the universe. That's what he said."

"I know what he said. But obviously, he hopes you'll succeed here."

"How can you know that?" Fitz asked. "Because he said so? Maybe he only meant that in the moment. Maybe he only means anything in the moment he says it, and nothing means anything beyond that."

"He's flying you out to the academy himself," his mother said, covering his hand with her own and leaning in until he met her eyes. "He took time off to do it. Would he do that if he didn't want you to succeed here?"

Fitz said nothing. His mother had never been in the foreign service, never been a diplomat or a guardian. Never been a cadet. She had no idea what it was going to be like for him after the rest of the school saw him stepping out of a private shuttle, and a top of the line private shuttle at that. She didn't know the words he'd hear spoken behind his back, just loud enough to reach his ears but not loud enough for him to pinpoint the speaker.

Well, it wasn't like he could make the other cadets like him less, anyway.

The shuttle landed on one of the strips, and it was—as it nearly always was—raining. The sky was gray, clouds billowing down as if longing to swallow up the ground below. The wind blew cold and relentless.

Fitz went to his cabin to grab his jacket and bag. Then he let his mother fuss over him, smoothing the shoulders of his uniform before helping him into his jacket, then turning him around to fuss with that too.

"Come on, mom," he said. "I'm later than everyone else already. I should've taken the intergalactic railway."

"We got more time together this way," she said, frowning as she adjusted his hat. "Is this thing warm enough?"

"Warm enough to get me inside the library doors," Fitz said. "I have to go."

"All right," she relented. She brushed imaginary lint off the front of his jacket before finally stepping back.

"Son," said his father from the cockpit doorway. Fitz bit back a cascade of commentary about his father's sudden appearance at the very last minute. None of those words would be helpful in his primary mission, which was getting off this shuttle.

Instead, he just gave his father a salute, a sincere gesture, his form as precise as he could make it: standing straight, shoulders back, hand just so.

His father returned the salute smartly, and Fitz was finally free to go.

"Stay in touch!" his mother called down the landing ramp after him.

"I will!" he promised. Then smirked to himself. Maybe he was like his father a little bit. Because in that moment, he meant it. But he was pretty sure tomorrow that promise would slide down to the bottom of his to-do list. By the end of the week, it wouldn't even make the list.

Fitz jogged across the wet field, trying to dodge the large raindrops, but not particularly successfully. The library windows were fogged up on the inside, but the light behind that fog was warm and inviting, and he could see the silhouettes of cadets moving around.

He paused inside the doorway for just a moment, long enough to sweep a gaze up and down the length of the room and satisfy himself that Ritchie wasn't there. There were other girls with brown hair cut short in almost the same style as she favored, but none of their hair had the right glow like honey even in the unflattering light of the library.

Fitz hitched the straps of his bag a little higher on his shoulder and crossed the foyer to the low-ceilinged but wide hallway that led to the barracks. He passed groups of cadets catching up after the break. Most ignored him, but one or two raised a chin at him in greeting as he passed. Fitz waggled the fingers of the hand that was holding the bag strap on his shoulder in return.

He had decided weeks ago when he arrived here that he was actually going to try this time, and the first semester hadn't gone badly at all. None of the instructors were giving him a hard time, and even the handful of cadets who knew him from other academies around the Union of Free Worlds let him be. If there was a whisper network of rumors about his past, he heard nothing of it. And by this much time in a new academy, he usually had.

But he hadn't made any friends either. Sure, he knew Ritchie, had since they were kids. And her buddy Moreau was someone he had crossed paths with at parties more than once, although he hadn't really gotten to know her until she had helped him and Ritchie solve the murder on the trip to the academy at the beginning of the year.

That had been wild.

But he hardly ever had more than a minute or two to speak with them, and then only when he hunted them down during free time or at meals. Even in classes they had together, they were seated too far apart for more than an exchange of glances.

He passed the cafeteria and took the corridor down his section of the barracks, then skipped down the flight of stairs that brought him several levels down below the classrooms and other meeting places.

Did they have to put the barracks in the deepest, coldest, dampest part of the complex? What he wouldn't give to wake up looking out a window at natural light just for once. And the excessive width of the hallways just made the low ceiling feel that much more smothering. The designer of this complex must have been some sort of sadist.

He passed the sophomore rec room, filled with more cadets milling about. Then the dampness kicked up a notch as he passed the open doorway to the showers, although the cold remained untouched. The sinks and toilets and every single tile on the floor, walls and ceiling gleamed brightly. The cleaning robots had clearly not been programmed to scale back their efforts while the cadets were away.

He expected by tomorrow morning nothing would like quite so shiny.

He left the cloying smell of cleaner behind as he stepped into the room where his bunk was. The smell here was staler, as if long-abandoned piles of unwashed gym clothes lurked just out of sight. But it was a comforting smell.

He looked around at the familiar room: two bunks and a desk on either side of the room. Both bunks on the right side were neatly made, both shelves over the desk holding tablets of various sizes and an array of knickknacks arranged just so. The left side of the room was just as neat, but only the bottom bunk was made. The top shelf over the desk was bare, the bottom boasting a single academy-issued tablet.

Fitz threw his bag on the bottom bunk on the left with a sigh, looking at the tightly rolled mattress and plastic-sealed bedding still sitting on the top bunk as if just about to be used at any moment.

Just like it had been all through his first semester.

Fitz turned away, taking off his jacket and hat and opening one of the four lockers that spanned the wall between the bunks.

"Hey, Fitz," someone said behind him. He turned to see his two roommates, Imhof and Stucki, coming in the door. But not just arriving back at the academy like he was; they were dressed in gym clothes, all red-faced and sweaty.

"Hey, Stucki," Fitz said. It was always Stucki who spoke to Fitz. Not that Imhof was shy. He just seemed to prefer to pretend Fitz wasn't there. "Good break?"

"Meh," he said with a wavering hand gesture indicating an equilibrium between boredom and interest had been found.

"Yeah, me too," Fitz said.

Imhof scoffed before crossing the room to fling open his own locker door.

"What's that?" Fitz asked, as if he had missed something Imhof had said.

"I didn't say anything," he said.

"Didn't you?" Fitz said, amused despite himself. "Because you seemed to doubt that I could ever experience an inter-semester break that could be described as, like Stucki said, 'meh.'"

"I'm not doubting anything," Imhof said, taking his shower bag out of the locker and slamming the door shut again. He gave Fitz what Fitz was sure was meant to be a pointed look before turning on his heel to march out of the room.

But whatever Imhof's point had been, Fitz had missed it.

"Ignore him," Stucki said, opening his own locker to fetch his shower bag. "We were up on the running track when you landed. Sweet shuttle, man. Was that a Mark 6?"

"Mark 7," Fitz said, hating the words but not able to hold them back. "The newest model."

"But that's not supposed to be out until next season," Stucki said, clearly impressed.

As Fitz's father surely intended everyone to be.

"Yeah, well," Fitz said, but just ended with a shrug.

"Is he picking you up again at the end of the semester?" Stucki asked.

"Gah, I hope not," Fitz said.

"Oh," Stucki said and looked so disappointed that Fitz almost felt bad for being so glib. "Too bad. I was going to work on you all semester to convince you to give me a tour."

Fitz watched Stucki head off after his buddy Imhof down the hall towards the showers. Then he turned his attention to his bag, opening it up and transferring item after item from it to the locker.

Still not really winning at this making friends thing. Too late to fix anything today. He had missed dinner and everything. He would have to do better tomorrow.

He accessed his implant and advanced his morning alarm by a few minutes. He had to get to the mess hall early if he wanted to catch Ritchie and Moreau. Maybe a few minutes with them at breakfast would put him in a friendlier place before going to class.

If only the academy would just fill that last opening and assign him a buddy already.

3

RITCHIE LONGED to linger in the warmth of the shower like she had done during the inter-semester break, but there were only eight showerheads for the dozens of cadets taking turns. She made one last pass to be sure all the soap was rinsed out of her hair, then stepped out of the water and made for the towel racks.

They were heated, which was nice. But the moment she stepped out of the shower area to brush her teeth at one of the sinks, the cold air hit her. That cold reminded her just how deep under the surface the barracks were. It just felt cavey. This was a cold that was never dispelled by the light of any sun. She focused on the tiled walls and floor, the metal sinks all in a row. Just like on any space station. No different.

The oppressive, trapped under a mountain feeling passed.

She brushed her teeth, then dried her hair and brushed it back from her face. It needed a trim, but she wouldn't have an opportunity to get one until the weekend. The bangs fell past her eyebrows but not quite into her eyes. She kept brushing it back until it stopped falling forward again, then had to be satisfied: the sinks had a line of waiting cadets the same as the showers did.

Ritchie snugged the towel around her, all of its warmth gone now, then headed out into the hallway, dodging a little robot on the floor that was desperately trying to wipe up wet footprints as quickly as the cadets were making them. She made her way down the hall to her room, passing several others full of chattering cadets getting dressed for the semester's first day of classes. She could smell coffee in the air, a rich dark roast. Someone was being bold about their contraband. Everyone knew the robot drones could detect such things, and they always reported them to the cadet captains.

Which in this wing of the barracks meant Jeger. And she was a serious stickler for the rules.

Ritchie shuddered at the thought of the tongue lashing someone was going to get this afternoon for sure. Because Jeger wouldn't pull the culprit aside, oh no. Public humiliation, that was Jeger's style.

Ritchie went in the open doorway to the room she shared with her buddy Moreau, plus two other sophomore cadets. Moreau was already in her flight suit and was sitting at the desk, idly turning pages in her reader. Cadet Frei was standing at the open door of her locker, fussing in the mirror. Her black hair was neatly plaited into dozens of neat braids, which she was arranging into a sizable bun at the back of her head. She was pressing it down onto her skull and pinning it in place so it wouldn't interfere with the fit of her flight helmet. Ritchie was glad she had cut off her own long hair, although hers had been nowhere near as thick as Frei's.

Frei's buddy Grof was bouncing on her toes. She was already dressed and ready to go, but as always, she had extra energy to burn off even before breakfast. Her own dark hair was a frizzy cloud that bounced just half a blink behind the bouncing of the rest of her. It was hypnotic.

"Morning," Grof said as Ritchie came in.

"Morning," Ritchie said, heading for her locker.

"Ready for the combat flight drill?" Grof asked, still bouncing. "Best way to get back into the flow, right? Just dive right in the deep end."

"I hope so," Ritchie said, pushing the hair back out of her eyes before pulling on her flight suit.

"You sound nervous," Grof said with a little frown.

"Do I?" Ritchie asked.

"Yes," Moreau said, not looking up from her tablet.

"I think I'm okay," Ritchie said, closing up the front of her suit, then reaching for her boots and socks.

"That doesn't sound very confident," Grof said. "You stayed over break to do all that extra training, right?" Ritchie nodded. "Well, what did Colonel Hansen say?"

"He said he's not a combat flight instructor," Ritchie said.

"Sounds like Hansen," Frei said, giving her hair one last adjustment then shutting her locker door.

"He said more than that," Moreau said, looking up at Ritchie over the top of her reader.

"Well, the last drill he ran at a higher difficulty than normal without telling me," Ritchie said. "And I did okay."

"Okay?" Grof said. "Either you beat the thing or you didn't."

"I did, but barely," Ritchie said.

Grof stopped bouncing to grab Ritchie by the shoulders and look her straight in the eyes. "These are combat drills. You either die or you don't. Who cares about barely?"

"Jeger," Moreau said.

"Exactly," Ritchie said, giving Moreau a nod of thanks. "It doesn't matter that I can successfully do a thing, not to Jeger. I have to do it flawlessly, or she'll find something to nitpick."

"That's her job," Grof said. "She's pushing you. It's not the most comfortable thing in the world, sure, but who cares? Use it."

Ritchie just stopped herself from biting down on her sore lip before giving Grof a nod.

But it was easy for Grof to say such things. Grof excelled at everything. More, she inspired everyone around her. Cadets on her team always performed better at any task than they expected to. Jeger got into everyone's face at some time or another, but never Grof.

And it's not like Jeger couldn't find a thing to go after if she wanted to. Grof's frizzy cloud of hair was well outside the bounds of regulations. But because of everything else she had going on, she apparently got a pass on the less important regulations.

"Ready for breakfast?" Moreau asked her as she set her reader aside.

"You bet," Ritchie said. "I want to find Fitz; I didn't see him when everyone disembarked from the railway yesterday."

"No, he flew in later on his private shuttle," Moreau said. Ritchie started to laugh, then realized Moreau was completely serious. "Yeah, we're going to have to ask him about that," Moreau said, and Ritchie could just picture Fitz squirming as Moreau grilled him about... actually, Ritchie didn't know what there was to ask him about flying in on a shuttle. But Moreau clearly had some things in mind.

"You can't go like that," Frei said.

"Like what?" Ritchie asked, running her hands over her flight suit then looking down at her boots. She was totally in uniform, nothing missing or out of place. There was not so much as a speck of dirt anywhere on her, not even her freshly polished boots.

But Frei was making a vague circling gesture around the top of Ritchie's head as she stood bent over to inspect the toes of her boots. Ritchie straightened up, tossing her hair back out of her eyes.

And knew at once what Frei was talking about.

"I'm going to get it cut this weekend," Ritchie said, covering her shaggy bangs with her hand.

"You should've had it done *last* weekend," Frei said.

"I know, I just didn't notice at the time," Ritchie said. "I was practicing and studying and not really looking in the mirror at all."

"I have scissors," Moreau said.

"No!" Grof said, catching Ritchie's arm as if to stop her from lunging for what Moreau offered. "Don't try to cut your own hair. I doubt you have the skills, and Jeger will be all over the results of that sort of failure."

"I have to do something," Ritchie said.

"Do you want some pins?" Frei asked, her hand on the handle of her locker.

"No, I've got something better," Grof said. She opened her locker and pulled open a drawer. She dug through a large collection of headbands and brushes and clips, all things Ritchie had never seen Grof use. Then she found what she was looking for, tossing a little white jar at Ritchie. Ritchie caught it, then turned it over in her hands, looking for a label.

There was none.

"What is it?" Ritchie asked.

"Styling paste," Grof said. "It's not as overwhelmingly thick as it sounds. Just rub it on your hands and work it through your hair. It will hold that swept-back look you've been trying for."

"Thanks," Ritchie said. Frei made an impatient sound in the back of her throat.

"Leave it on my bunk when you're done," Grof said, walking backwards towards the doorway where her buddy was waiting.

"Will do," Ritchie said. Then she turned to Moreau. "You should go to breakfast; don't wait for me."

"Are you sure?" Moreau asked. "I don't mind waiting until you're done."

"No, go find Fitz for me," Ritchie said. "I'll catch up with both of you in just a minute."

"I'll grab a plate of eggs for you," Moreau said as they both headed for the doorway. "You don't want to be late to formation; Jeger doesn't need that kind of ammo against you on day one. But you can't skip breakfast, either. You get fuzzy-headed when you try it."

"I know," Ritchie said. "Coffee too?" she added. The smell of that particular contraband was still lingering in the hallway.

"I thought that went without saying," Moreau said. Then they parted ways, Moreau heading up towards the mess hall and Ritchie jogging back to the bathrooms. Every barracks room she passed was empty, and the only sound was her own clomping boots. The little cleaning robot was tracing a zig-zagging path in front of the showers, although not a single wet footprint remained. The air was still damp, but it was a cold damp now, not a steamy one.

Ritchie headed straight to the sinks, screwing off the top of the jar as she walked. She sniffed at the shiny white contents. Coconut. Nice. She scooped out a bit and set the jar on the ledge in front of the mirror before rubbing the paste between her hands. Somewhere she could hear a faucet dripping and looked up and down the row of sinks. None of them were dripping; it must be coming from one of the showers. Still rubbing her hands, Ritchie started to cross the room towards the showers, but stopped when she heard voices coming from inside.

Someone was running even later than she was, or rather two some-ones. And yet the dripping sound had been drop after drop striking tile, not a running shower. These two someones hadn't overslept, then. They had gone to one of the few places where it was possible to have a conversation without a bunch of other cadets overhearing it.

Ritchie froze in her steps. If someone wanted a quick moment's privacy, who was she to intrude?

Surely they had heard her come in; she hadn't made any attempt to walk softly, and even setting the jar on the ledge had made a clatter. But even so, she made an effort to be silent as she crept back to the mirror to quickly finish slicking back her hair. The warmth of her hands had softened what had felt like too thick of a paste, and it was transferring from her hands to her hair without unsightly clumps. But it wasn't distributing evenly, and she had to keep running her hands through it over and over again, covering every part of her head.

The voices were growing louder from the half-whispers she had heard before. They were drowning out the sound of the drip now, although she still couldn't make out any specific words. But the tone was telling. One person was ending everything on an up note, as if earnestly making points they were hoping would be agreed with. But the other person's responses were clipped short, and Ritchie was pretty sure they were negatory.

Ritchie ran her hands more quickly through her hair, sweeping it back from her forehead in a sort of pompadour look. It was working. She teased a last few strands into place, then gave her head a test shake. Her hair moved, but only a little bit. She stopped, shaking her head. It looked exactly the way she had arranged it. Perfect.

She started to reach for the jar but realized her hands were quite sticky. She stuck them under the faucet. In the split second before the water started flowing, she heard one of the two people in the showers.

"You tell him or I will!"

The voice was familiar, but Ritchie couldn't quite place it. She soaped her hands, hoping to grab the jar and make herself scarce, but the paste was tenacious. She scrubbed harder. The voices were still going, but with the water running, she was once again left to interpret tone without being able to make out any words.

Finally, her hands were clean, and she pulled them out from under the water to run them through the dryer.

"Let. It. Go."

Now that voice was familiar. Jeger. Her hands weren't quite dry, but Ritchie didn't care. She snatched up the jar and lid and turned to run for it, but quickly turned back to the mirror as she saw Jeger marching out of the showers.

Ritchie stood frozen, hunched over the jar in her hands as if she could will herself invisible. Jeger would surely assume Ritchie had been there to eavesdrop. She wouldn't believe anything Ritchie would say to the contrary. And the last thing Ritchie needed was to give Jeger an actual reason to hate her.

She realized her whole body was tensed up, waiting for the blow of Jeger's shouted demands for an explanation, a blow that hadn't come. She forced herself to relax, glancing up in the mirror just in time to see Jeger disappear out into the hallway, striding off in the direction of the mess hall.

Had Jeger not even seen her there? That was maybe too much to hope for, but if she was going to pretend like Ritchie wasn't there, Ritchie could pretend the same. No reason to ever mention what she hadn't, in fact, even heard.

But that curious part of her mind was already churning. Who was this "him" the other voice had spoken of? What did he need to be told?

Ritchie remembered there was still one person left in the showers. She debated hiding in the toilets, but she was late enough already. She set her shoulders back and walked towards the doorway, trying for both speed and silence.

She failed at both.

"Cadet!" the person in the shower said in a commanding voice. Ritchie froze, reluctant to turn around. But she didn't need to. The other cadet came out of the showers and circled around Ritchie to stand between her and the safety of the wide hallway.

"Cadet..." Ritchie said, straining to remember the name. She glanced down at the tag on the front of the other cadet's flight suit. "Egli," she finished.

Oh yes, Egli. Another final year cadet. A cadet lieutenant, actually.

Jeger's assigned buddy. Now she was really curious what they had been arguing about. Why were they doing it here and not in their own barracks?

"Ritchie, right?" Egli asked.

"Yes," Ritchie said. "Just dealing with a hair issue." She held out the jar, which being without any sort of label in no way backed up her story.

Egli raised a single eyebrow but said nothing.

"Yes," Ritchie said again. "Just heading for breakfast now before it's too late."

"Breakfast," Egli said, as if it were a new concept to her.

"So I'm just going to go," Ritchie said, and Egli finally seemed to realize she was blocking Ritchie's way. She stepped aside with a sweeping gesture of one arm.

But there was something on her face, a line of worry between her eyebrows, a tightness to her jaw. Ritchie stayed where she was.

"Is everything all right?" she asked.

"Fine," Egli said, a short, dismissive word.

"Because I didn't hear what you were saying just now, but you both seemed upset," Ritchie said. "Is there something I can do?"

"Get to the cafeteria," Egli said. This time, her arms were gesturing as if she hoped to sweep Ritchie away. "You have more than enough problems of your own to deal with, I should think. No need to stick your nose around hunting for more."

Ritchie felt her cheeks flushing darkly, but said nothing. She jogged down the hallway, stopping at the doorway to her barracks to toss the jar onto Grof's mostly made bunk. Then she broke into a run to get to the cafeteria before it was too late.

Egli was right; it was none of her business. And she was right that Ritchie had more than enough problems of her own, although she didn't think offering help merited such an unkind response.

But still. Who was this "him?"

4

FITZ GOT to the mess hall so early they weren't even ready to serve food yet. He took a position to one side of the main door and watched the trickle of cadets grow into a thick onslaught and then dwindle back down to a trickle.

He had expected Ritchie to be among the first. In fact, he expected despite his own extra early arrival to find her already there, perhaps studying at a table while she waited for service to start. She was always early for everything, and that went double for times when she couldn't possibly be behind because she had stayed to ask extra questions at the end of the class before.

A sudden, horrid thought struck him. Had she not come back from break for some reason? But no, she had said she wasn't even going home for the break. She wanted to log more glider hours, she had said, but he had suspected that the journey home and back again wasn't something her family could easily afford.

Then he saw Moreau walking towards him, recognizable even at a distance by the tall topknot of blonde hair set at the very apex of her skull. It must be a bit of a trick, getting a helmet down over that.

"Hey," she said when she was close enough for him to hear her.

"Hey," he said. "Where's Ritchie?"

Moreau rolled her eyes. "She's not quite perfect. But she'll be along in a minute."

"She's going to attain perfection in a minute?" he asked.

"Well, it's just a hair thing," Moreau said, gesturing around her own head as if that explained something. "It's a tad out of regulation."

Now Fitz rolled his eyes. "Who cares? I mean, besides Ritchie."

"Jeger," Moreau said, keeping her voice low and looking around in case the cadet captain in question was within earshot.

"Oh, yeah. Of course," Fitz said. Jeger did enjoy busting Ritchie for any possible infraction. He knew Ritchie wouldn't appreciate him speaking on her behalf, so he had bitten his tongue every time he had seen Jeger have Ritchie run extra laps, or make her reassemble a weapon Jeger had torn apart for some minuscule grease speck that had probably never even existed, or making her drop and do pushups for nothing at all.

The irony left a bitter taste in his mouth. He, who even though he was actually trying this time around, still messed up stuff all the time, did not get busted even half as much as Ritchie did. Ritchie, who had come to the academy insanely eager to please, whose attitude had never flagged, who was working twice as hard as the rest of them because she had gaps in her education the others didn't have, could never catch a break with a certain cadet captain.

Would it kill Jeger to try a little encouragement once in a while? Was hardcore discipline really what Ritchie needed?

"They're closing down the line," Moreau said. "I'll sneak something into my pockets for Ritchie, I guess. You coming?"

"No," Fitz said, suddenly not remotely hungry. "I'll see you on the hangar deck."

"Sure thing," Moreau said and hustled to grab a tray before they were gone.

Fitz thrust his hands into the pockets of his flight suit and walked away from the mess hall. He kept his steps slow, still hoping to see Ritchie running up from the barracks, but there was no sign of her. When that corridor off the main hallway was behind him, he picked up his pace, crossing the library to head outside.

The sun was shining down through many breaks in the high cloud cover, and it looked like it was going to be as perfect a day as Oymyakon ever had. The clouds were whitish-gray and wispy, crossing the sky at a lazy pace. Fair weather would make for easier flying, which actually wasn't an advantage for him in combat flight. Fitz had been flying a glider of his own back on his homeworld since he was tall enough to reach all the controls at the age of eight. He hadn't practiced combat maneuvers, but he had flown in all sorts of weather despite his mother's objections. In foul weather, his fellow cadets had a harder time executing the maneuvers they had so carefully studied on the ground. Fitz, with his lifelong practice, had the advantage then.

But in fair weather, he was constantly getting shot down in the first seconds of every simulation. Mainly because he had never studied any of the maneuvers. He should probably remedy that, but he really hated studying something rather than simply doing it.

He had just concluded that the first day of the semester was going to be a wash for him when he stepped out of the outer doors and into the fresh air, and the pressure on his ears changed so fast it was actually painful.

Low pressure. Very low pressure. He shaded his eyes from the sun and peered around the sky. Everything still looked calm, except for directly behind the academy building. It was harder to see in that direction since the mountain peak obscured the view, but the sky was definitely darker there. Darker, and almost still. A storm was hovering there, building in intensity but not advancing. Not yet.

Depending on when that got moving, the combat flight exercise might get very interesting indeed.

Fitz jogged along the gravel trail across the open field to the entrance to the hangar. Like the hallways in the academy proper, this one was wide with a low ceiling. It angled down to the hangar level, and he quickly left the warmth of the sun behind.

The hangar deck was mostly dark, lit only by the dim emergency lighting that traced out paths of egress, but the moment he reached the end of the low hallway, the systems detected him there and turned on the overhead lights one by one. Fitz crossed the space and headed directly to his own assigned glider.

He remembered when he had been told that he was being transferred to this academy, when he had first seen its name on the screen of his reader. He had to look up on a map just where the planet Oymyakon was located. That had required several zooms out before it finally appeared on the edge of the map centered on the heart of the Union of Free Worlds. And he had thought, well, yeah, it was very far away from anything at all, but how bad could it be? It was still a Union of Free Worlds Foreign Service Academy. That had to mean something.

He looked at the sad little glider before him and sighed. Nope. It meant pretty much nothing at all. Granted, none of the gliders he had flown at the other academies had been anything like the state-of-the-art one he had at home. But the gliders here were so old he didn't know how they could still be considered safe to fly. Some of them were barely holding together. He put a hand on the wing of his own craft and starting his walk-around inspection.

There was something in the air, some sickly sweet odor too faint for him to quiet identify. He didn't know where it was coming from, except that it wasn't from his own glider. Probably not any of the other gliders either; they were so mechanically simple they were barely more than kites. He wondered if it came from the few shuttles that were parked a few hundred meters further down. Or perhaps the ground vehicles just as far away in the other direction. The smell was too faint for him to tell.

Well, either way, not his problem.

He was just making his way towards the nose of his glider when he heard voices coming from the direction of the ground vehicles. He ducked under the nose to take a look. No one had been on the hangar deck when he'd come down, or the lights would have been illuminated already. But there wasn't a passageway to the surface on that side of the deck, either. Those were all on this side, the one closer to the surface.

Then two cadets came into view from around the tires of a personnel carrier. He immediately recognized the yellowish-blonde hair cut in a cap-style that was exactly regulation in length. Jeger. The other cadet had dark hair in tight twists close to his head. Bale, the other cadet captain. They must have been in the command room, which was out of his view behind the parked vehicles. And they must have been in there for some time, since the lights had gone out on the deck. But that was hardly remarkable; they were probably meeting to discuss how they were going to handle the first combat flight exercise of the semester.

Fitz turned his attention back to his glider, as spotless as he had left it before break. He finished his walk around, then crouched to get underneath it.

He could hear Bale and Jeger arguing as they drew nearer. Surely they knew he was there. The command room was all glass on the side that looked out on the hangar deck. They would've seen the lights come back on when Fitz came down the hallway.

But when he finished his inspection of the bottom of his glider he lingered, bent over uncomfortably, because he had a strong suspicion that they didn't realize he was there. Especially as they drew closer, and he could hear their words.

"How many times do we have to have this same conversation, Bale?" Jeger said and stopped walking to turn to face Bale. Right in front of the nose of Fitz's glider.

"Probably for the rest of this year, don't you think?" Bale said. While Jeger was spitting the words out and leaning in to get inside Bale's personal space, Bale's words were calm. He even offered her a smile as he lifted his hands, palms up, towards the ceiling or perhaps the sky above. "What else can I do?"

"Let this go?" she snapped.

"Maybe I could, if I felt like you were hearing me," Bale said.

"That's a lie," Jeger said. "You won't let this go until I agree to do things your way."

"I'm not saying that," Bale said. "You are who you are. And that's a good thing."

Jeger scoffed and rolled her eyes.

"Hey, I mean that," Bale said. "Being cadet captain is something you earned a hundred times over, okay? I know that. And you earned it by being a hardass, right?"

"Better too hard than too soft," Jeger said, clearly not taking what he said remotely like a compliment.

"Those aren't the only choices," Bale said. "And being a little more encouraging isn't the same as being soft."

Jeger narrowed her eyes at him, then spun on her heel to walk away. Bale rushed to get ahead of her.

"I'm not even saying meet me halfway," he said, walking backward when it became clear Jeger wasn't going to stop. "Just ease up a little. Measure out the discipline."

Jeger stopped so abruptly that Bale took several more steps backward before dancing forward again to stand in front of her.

"You know what's coming," she said, now speaking so low that Fitz had to creep a bit closer to catch her words.

"No one knows what's coming," Bale said.

"Maybe not exactly," she said. "Not how the specific players are going to line up, but the generalities are clear."

"Now, you know we don't agree on that either," Bale said, injecting just a hint of good-naturedness into his tone, probably to counteract some darker look in Jeger's eyes. Fitz couldn't tell, since her back was to him, but her posture was about as tense as it was possible to get. "War is not inevitable. I'm not even sure it's the most likely outcome."

"It is," Jeger said. "I've shown you everything I've seen, and if you can't put the pieces together to see the big picture, I guess I can't help you."

"There's more than one way to arrange those pieces," Bale said. "And like I said before, there are pieces you ignore that should be part of your big picture. And some of your pieces, I'd argue, don't have the importance you've assigned to them. The Yuffid, for instance."

Fitz's breath caught. Like it always did when someone mentioned that particular species. The Yuffid had creeped him out even before they had taken Ritchie's father and left Union space, never to return or communicate with Union diplomats again.

"Say I'm wrong, then," Jeger said, throwing up her hands. "Say your view is right, and nothing ever comes to anything. Then doing things my way is going to turn out the best class of cadets this academy has ever seen for no reason. They'll still be the best, even doing the same routine tasks that diplomats and guardians are doing now.

"But if you're wrong," she said, leaning forward to punch a finger into Bale's chest. "If you're wrong, and there is war, this class of cadets will be *ready* for it. They'll be hard and disciplined and prepared for anything."

Bale said nothing, and Jeger let her arm drop back to her side. She started to walk away again but then stopped to say over her shoulder, "but I'm right, and we do things your way? They won't be ready for anything. They'll still want cheerleaders encouraging them on while they falter through the most basic of tasks. And then they'll be dead. Me demanding the best of everyone isn't going to end up with anyone dead. Can you say the same of your training methods?"

Then she turned and stalked off, not waiting for the answer that Bale didn't seem to have, anyway.

Bale remained in the middle of the hangar deck, looking down at the toes of his boots and tugging at his bottom lip, lost in thought.

He didn't look like he ever intended to move, but Fitz couldn't stay bent over under the glider anymore. He slipped out and stretched his back. Something popped in a satisfying way, and Fitz must've let out a sigh of relief because Bale was now looking up at him.

"Hey," Fitz said. "Just doing a preflight."

"How is it?" Bale asked, walking up to touch the glider's wing. Then he wrinkled his nose. "What's that smell?"

"Something's leaking fluid," Fitz said. "It might be from one of the shuttles, but I think the ground vehicles are more likely."

"I'll have to report it," Bale said, still sniffing the air.

"For what it's worth, I think you're right," Fitz said. Bale gave him a questioning look, and Fitz was forced to go on. "About Jeger. And her training techniques. Can't you take it up with Command?"

Bale's face went hard, and Fitz wished he had never as much as admitted to eavesdropping. "That's not your business, cadet."

"Isn't it everybody's business?" Fitz countered. Bale's gaze darkened further. "I mean, when she crushes some poor cadet's spirit, that affects all of us. We have to build them back up again."

"That's part of the point of it," Bale said. "When it's just you and your team, being able to be there for each other will matter."

"Sure," Fitz agreed. "But what should be demoralizing us shouldn't be coming from our own side, should it?"

Bale's anger dissipated slightly. "Well, that's true as far as it goes. But there isn't anything here but our side. Part of being a cadet captain is putting yourself outside of the rest of the group, to be that external stimulus. For the good of the group."

"Sounds lonely," Fitz said.

"Sometimes it is," Bale admitted with a shrug. "Between you and me, I'm looking forward to next year when I'm a lowly novice cadet all over again, just at a bigger school."

"I can see why," Fitz said. At Bale's questioning look, he added, "well, even admirals have other admirals to commiserate with about the stresses of command or whatever. But all you have is Jeger?"

"She's not that bad," Bale said. "You caught us at a bad moment."

Fitz decided not to mention that he'd heard earlier in the conversation when Jeger had been complaining about how many times they'd had that conversation already. How many bad moments had there been between them? Compared to how many good?

"She is that bad," Fitz said instead, but his tone was light, not serious. "Admit it."

"I won't," Bale said, but he was grinning now.

"She is," Fitz said. "Think of all the enemies she's made since she came to this academy. Heck, that's probably why she feels like a war is coming. Who wouldn't be a little paranoid under those circumstances?"

"She's fine," Bale said again.

A chatter of voices drew their attention to the bottom of the hallway, where the first of the cadets were emerging fresh from breakfast.

"Duty calls," Bale said. "I don't suppose I need to tell you to keep what you heard to yourself?"

"Of course you don't," Fitz said, fighting the urge to cross his fingers behind his back as he said the words.

As if there was any chance he wasn't going to share something so juicy with Ritchie and Moreau.

5

RITCHIE STOOD at attention beside the nose of her glider, in a line with all the other cadets and their gliders. Jeger was working her way down the line, looking over the gliders, the cadets' preflight checklists, and the cadets themselves. Ritchie resisted the temptation to keep looking down the line to see how far Jeger had progressed, how close she was drawing to Ritchie herself. Being caught looking around while in formation was the last thing she needed.

But there was a flutter of motion just at the edge of her peripheral vision. Someone waving? She didn't dare turn her head, but she looked in that direction.

Fitz. Of course it was Fitz. He lowered his half-raised hand the moment he saw her looking back at him, and neither Jeger nor Bale seemed to have noticed. Then he raised it again, just a bit, to give her a thumbs up. As if that were discreet given the over-sized grin on his face.

A smile threatened to turn the corners of her mouth up, but the urge disappeared in a flash at the sound of Jeger's raised voice. Ritchie wasn't her target, not yet. One of the other cadets' palms slapped onto the deck as she counted out pushups for some small infraction.

Jeger continued her methodical inspection, but Bale was already done with his and was waiting at the end of the line of gliders. Jeger gave the next handful of cadets a cursory look over before finally stopping in front of Ritchie.

"Preflight," Jeger said, and Ritchie handed over her tablet. Jeger glanced over it, then at the glider, before turning her eyes to Ritchie.

Ritchie fought the urge to reach up and make sure her hair wasn't starting to fall forward. Was that a loose lock she felt brushing against her forehead, or was she just imagining it?

The moment felt like it stretched on forever, Ritchie fighting not to squirm under Jeger's glare. But then Jeger just thrust the tablet back into Ritchie's hands and turned to Bale with a tight nod.

"Cadets, roll out!" Bale called, and everyone ran to get into their gliders.

Ritchie settled into her seat, strapping in, then putting on her helmet and lowering the visor. A sidebar on the holographic display showed her the names of the other cadets as they did the same. Then the names started sorting themselves into two columns of text in different colors, half in red and half in blue.

So they weren't going to fly together against a virtual opponent. They were going to fly against each other. Ritchie started to bite her lip but stopped herself, pressing her lips together tightly instead. She had hoped to ease in doing the same sorts of missions she had been practicing over the break, but she wasn't exactly surprised that Jeger wanted them to get back up to speed straight away.

She glanced down the lists of names. This wasn't particularly important information; she would see which gliders were friends and which were foes by the color her helmet's visor would project over them. And it was a randomly generated assignment; no clues to personal feelings in which names were where.

She was in Bale's squadron, not Jeger's. And so was Moreau, but not Fitz.

Ritchie felt the glider beneath her starting to move, being towed over to the elevator and then lifted up to be attached to the launch catapult. Ritchie's fingers on the yoke twitched ever so slightly as she imagined the movements she would be executing in just a few seconds.

Memories pressed at the back of her mind, eager to jump to the forefront and play a greatest hits of the number of times she had nearly crashed at the moment of launch, or nearly hit another glider. She pushed the visions back. She knew they weren't going to happen now. She had practiced too much to fall victim to any of those dangers again. But it was almost like she could feel Jeger watching her, waiting for her to fail, anyway.

Then her instrument panel beeped the countdown, just three beeps, and she was firing through the air like a missile.

The air that had seemed tranquil when she had walked out to the hangar was choppy now and got choppier as her altitude got higher. But she kept her glider's flight steady, and when her momentum was spent, she banked and flew out of the launch zone, following the circle through the sky that was lit up by her visor's hologram.

"Nice one, Ritchie," Bale's voice said in her ear. If Jeger had also been watching, she kept her assessment to herself.

Soon enough, all the gliders were in the sky, banking and circling as they awaited the command to attack.

"Blue Squadron, let's blast those red birds!" Bale said, and Ritchie, who had been watching for potential targets even as she floated through the clouds, immediately dove down to get on someone's six.

There was no room for anxiety in Ritchie's mind now. There was just line up a shot, take a shot, get away without being shot. A few near misses zipped past her wings, but she hit most of what she shot at. When she scored a hit, the hologram in her visor displayed the same convincing explosion effect it did when she was flying against entirely fictional opponents. After the explosion faded, that particular glider would be invisible through her and anyone else's visors who were still part of the simulated combat.

It was a little too convincing. Ritchie had a sick feeling in her stomach at the idea of shooting down her fellow cadets. But it was just an exercise. There was no reason it should be more disturbing than hand to hand practice when she had actually hurt at least one fellow cadet by punching her square in the nose. This was all fake.

But still. Disturbing.

The number of gliders still visible around her was dwindling. Not only was her team not winning, they weren't even staying competitive.

Alarms rang out, and Ritchie saw a glider drop into position behind her. She pulled up so abruptly she nearly lost control of her glider. If the wind started tossing her around...

"Sloppy move, Ritchie," Jeger said through the comm. Ritchie didn't answer, mostly because she was still fighting to get her shaking glider back under control, but also because Jeger wasn't her squadron leader and wasn't entitled to a response from her.

Seriously, why was she hearing from Jeger now and not Bale? Was Bale already out of it? Even if he were, Jeger was on the other team. She shouldn't be speaking to Ritchie while she was flying for the other team. Only the fact that she was a cadet captain let her do that.

The alarms went off again. Ritchie kept calm this time. Perhaps a shade too calm, as the shot from Jeger's glider zipped mere centimeters away from the cockpit window. The moisture beading there hissed as it boiled away, and Ritchie felt a frisson of fear. Was it necessary for the hologram to be that accurate?

Ritchie dove into a cloud, knowing that when it was dense enough around her, she would disappear from Jeger's view. She just needed a moment to gain a bit of altitude and get the upper hand.

She needed a breath of wind to buoy her up.

There was plenty of wind, but it was rushing around in chaotic directions, and Ritchie realized that a storm was about to break out all around them. Would the lesson be called off for the day?

By procedure, it should be. But Ritchie doubted it would until Jeger had one last kill. That kill being Ritchie.

Ritchie was still waiting for the needed wind when her alarms went off again. She banked, but the wind picked up, and her bank became an out-of-control tumble. She heard a loud yelling and belatedly realized it was coming from her.

She fought to stay calm, then fought her glider back to level flight.

And immediately, the alarms went off again.

Ritchie, calm gone, said every curse she knew in every language she knew how to curse in, some human and some not.

"Bye-bye, Ritchie," Jeger said in her ear. "You're still just not good enough."

Ritchie maneuvered again, hoping that Jeger's need to speak would slow her down just enough for Ritchie to escape again.

The alarms sounding around her didn't cease. But they weren't loud enough to drown out the sound of Jeger's laughter.

Laughter that ended in a yelp of surprise.

The alarms stopped, but Ritchie couldn't tell what had just happened. She pulled up and rolled over until she was facing the other way. She could see the red outline of Jeger's glider as she recovered from a wild tumble, but the only other glider in the sky was also red.

"Fitz! We're on the same team!" Jeger shrieked.

"Oh, yeah. Sorry about that," he said over the comm. The all-channels comm he shouldn't have access to as a lowly cadet.

Ritchie could hear the smile in his voice. So could everyone else. He wasn't fooling anyone.

"You and I are going to have words when we're back down on the ground," Jeger snarled.

"Yes, cadet captain," Fitz said, not bothering to sound remotely contrite.

"Get down on the ground with the others now," Jeger said. "I'll finish this last one myself."

"Roger," Fitz said.

Ritchie frowned. She really shouldn't be hearing communications over their squadron's channel. She glanced at her instrument panel, not sure how Fitz could have patched her in while they were both riding the wind kilometers up in the air, but not willing to bet he hadn't found a way. But no, she wasn't hearing their private conversation from their squadron's assigned channel.

Did Jeger not realize she had put them both on the public channel? Or was something else going on?

A different alarm rang through the cockpit, and Ritchie had to amend her earlier thought. They weren't kilometers off the ground anymore. She banked away from the mountain peak whose proximity had set off the alarm, then followed a gust of wind around to hunt for Jeger.

She didn't see any red gliders out there, or blue ones either. It sure looked like only the two of them were still aloft. Actually, it looked like Ritchie was alone, but she knew that couldn't possibly be true. Jeger would never land without taking her out first.

Her eyes scanned the horizon over and over again, trying to penetrate further into the darkening clouds around her. Every second that ticked by added to her anxiety, her certainty that while she couldn't see Jeger, Jeger definitely had eyes on her.

Then something burst out of a cloud formation in front of her and slightly to the left. Jeger wasn't even trying to maneuver behind her and take her out the easy way. She was storming in with a frontal assault.

Normally they were discouraged from trying for those, but Ritchie didn't think Jeger was taking much of a risk at all. Judging from the angle of her glider, she had Ritchie in her sights already. But Ritchie was too far to the right to get a shot in with her fixed-position laser cannon.

And the wind wasn't cooperating.

Ritchie tensed up, waiting for the shot to come. As stomach-churningly real as the explosion effects were when she shot someone down, it was a thousand times worse to be on the other end, feeling like your glider was exploding all around you. But there was nothing she could do until the wind changed.

It was like she could feel Jeger's finger touching the trigger. Tightening in the gentlest of squeezes.

Why was she waiting? Did she want to see Ritchie's face when she took her out? In another second or two, she'd be close enough to do it.

Ritchie cried out in alarm as something zoomed past her, blasting a path between her glider and Jeger's.

Fitz again. Was he nuts? The tip of his wing had all but grazed her windscreen.

"Take your shot!" he bellowed, and Ritchie realized that in his wake, she was now lined up with her target in her sights, and Jeger wasn't.

She took her shot.

Ritchie cried out in joy, thrusting her fists in the air as the holographic explosion filled her visor. Jeger had been so close the effect was blinding, but she refused to shut her eyes against it.

Jeger would make sure she paid for this victorious moment later. She and Fitz both. But in this moment, it was so worth it.

But while she was cheering, she heard a rising chatter of voices over the comms. She quieted, but everyone was talking over each other too much for her to grasp what the problem was.

"Stars! She's going to crash!" someone said, their voice breaking through a lull in overlapping conversations. Then everyone fell silent.

Ritchie spun her head in every direction. Had her proximity detectors failed on her? But they had detected that mountain peak earlier.

No, she wasn't the one who was crashing.

Jeger?

But Jeger had counted as a kill. The holographic projector in Ritchie's visor had hidden her glider from view from the moment that the fake explosion had faded away.

Ritchie slapped her visor up, then looked again.

At first, she saw nothing but clouds, heavy rain-laden clouds pressing down close on the mountains below. She could just make out the outlines of the academy facade where it jutted out of the mountainside.

She was losing momentum. The light flashing on her instrument panel was instructing her to find the nearest landing strip, the flashing increasing in frequency when she didn't respond. It would alarm in another second if she didn't turn her glider.

Ritchie banked and turned back towards the landing area.

She had just lined up with the landing strip when she saw another glider some ways off to her left. It was going down too fast and nowhere near the landing area.

It was going to nosedive straight into the rocky terrain on a neighboring mountainside. And there was nothing Ritchie could do.

The minute her wheels hit the ground, she undid her restraints and got up as much as she could out of her seat, ignoring the blare of alarms as she strained to find the spot where the glider must have gone down.

The clouds obligingly parted, but there was no sign of Jeger's glider. Was she in the air still? Had she pulled off some miraculous maneuver, caught a rogue wind to get just enough altitude to avoid the mountain?

Ritchie had seen Jeger do some spectacular things in a glider. But sometimes spectacular just wasn't enough.

"Please," Ritchie said, as her glider connected with the towing system with a hard lurch, and the alarms finally fell silent. "Please, let her be okay."

But her gut told her that Jeger was very far from okay.

6

FITZ SAW EVERYTHING. But what he saw made no sense. It couldn't be real. And yet he knew it was.

Because he had removed his visor minutes before. He knew this was no hologram.

He had needed to shut off the visor with all of its holographic information. It was designed not to let him do things like fly straight into other cadets' gliders, especially the ones on his own squad. So he had pushed it up out of his way before he'd even made his last run at Jeger.

Jeger, who had sent the signal to his glider that locked out the controls. She surely thought that meant Fitz could do nothing but follow her orders and land with the others. But it had taken him half a second to disable that. He knew the glider instrument panels backward and forwards, but he in no way needed them to fly.

Nothing but his own eyes and judgment had guided him through that last risky maneuver. Jeger saw him coming and had time to dodge out of his way, but he had been just off of Ritchie's six. Not close enough to set her alarms off, not that they would now that the combat training system had him marked as offline, but in her blind spot all the same. She had no warning before he appeared out of nowhere to just avoid brushing up against her glider as he dove past.

He supposed that had been, technically, an unacceptable risk. The slightest change in the wind and both their gliders would've fallen to the ground in a twisting mass. But it hadn't registered as a risk to him at all. He knew exactly how it would play out.

He had caught another wind and sailed back up into the sky as he told Ritchie to take her shot.

It was quite startling when he heard the zap of laser fire. His visor was off; the system disengaged. He was no longer part of the combat simulation. He shouldn't be hearing a thing at all.

Then the wind carried him around to where he could see both of their gliders. Ritchie's was rocking a bit as she took both hands off the yoke to raise them in celebration.

Jeger's was falling out of the sky, one wing a smoking ruin no longer capable of holding her aloft.

Ritchie's cries of victory over the comm told Fitz that she definitely wasn't seeing what he was. But then other voices popped up on the public channel, cadets asking each other if what they were seeing was real. The combat over with the last red fighter down, all channels were now public.

Fitz gripped his yoke and brought his glider down, chasing Jeger. Even at a distance, he could tell she wasn't panicking. She was keeping her nose up, struggling to control her descent.

Landing with one wing missing was nearly impossible on a good day. And as another gust of wind rocked his glider, Fitz knew this was pretty far from a good day.

Jeger had slowed her descent enough that Fitz managed to pull alongside her.

He could see her through the cockpit windscreen. Her helmet had been knocked askew, and there was a frightening amount of blood running down the side of her face. She hadn't secured the strap, some absurd part of his mind noted. She would've destroyed any other cadet she caught flying in that condition.

Then she looked over at him, just a glance, but it was enough. They both knew there was nothing she could do. She was going to crash. And the only thing ahead of her was the rocky side of one of the mountain peaks they could see from the library windows.

And there was nothing he could do to help. Not a thing.

And she was so very afraid.

He raised a hand in salute, but her eyes were closed now. She had let go of the yoke. Her glider, barely in control when she was actively flying it, started to spin.

Fitz pulled up just before they reached the mountainside. But this mountain peak was like a spire, steep and narrow. The winds dancing around it were chaotic, and with his momentum gone, he was running out of options.

He couldn't see what had happened to Jeger. But if he wasn't careful, he was going to crash himself.

He darted around the tall prominence of the bare stone peak, circling around the mountain itself. Rocky outcroppings were passing less than a meter below his lowered wheels. He was going down, and there was nowhere clear to land.

Then he saw it. An alpine meadow, barely the size of a modest family's yard back home. It wasn't much, but it was his only chance.

Fitz slammed down all of his flaps just as the tailwind shifted to a headwind. He hung in the sky for a moment, as if the glider couldn't figure out what it wanted to do. Then he slammed down to the ground, almost perfectly centered in the little meadow.

The moment his wheels were on the ground, Fitz was out of the cockpit. The icy wind sucked his breath away. He saw the academy far below him on the next mountain through a momentary break in the clouds. Then it was gone. Then he looked the other way, higher up his own mountain.

At first, all he could see were swirling clouds flowing past the peak, the sharp stony face cutting through those clouds like a knife through cotton. Then he realized part of that wasn't cloud. It was smoke.

He scrambled over the rocks as quickly as he could, climbing over boulders then picking his way over screes of loose rock.

So much smoke. When the wind shifted just the right way, he could smell it. Burning glider fuselage, a chemical smell. The instruments, a more electrical sort of burning smell.

Finally, he scrambled over one last ridge and saw the remains of the glider still burning hotly. The ice-cold wind only seemed to be whipping it up into a brighter frenzy. Fitz ran towards it, but the heat was too intense. He could feel his eyelashes singeing.

He could smell Jeger.

"No, no, no, no," Fitz said over and over, then threw an arm across his eyes and tried again to force himself closer to the glider. She couldn't be dead. She couldn't be.

Not that being trapped in there was a better option. Just the thought had him pressing on, even though he was sure some of what he was smelling was his own hair starting to smolder.

Then something pulled him back. Or rather, someone.

"Cadet!" they yelled as they pulled him back out of the heat. He couldn't see who it was, but he guessed it was the emergency medical team from the academy, who would've been observing the flight combat exercise from the ground. The uniform had no name tag, but the two snakes wrapped around a staff on the person's breast pocket said he was right.

Person. He couldn't even tell if it was a man or woman under all that protective gear.

The person dragged him back to the last ridge and shoved him until he sat down on a flattish boulder. "Stay down," they said, their voice distorted by their protective helmet. "We'll take care of her."

"It's too late," Fitz said, dragging his arm across his eyes. Where had he lost his helmet?

"Maybe not," they said. But Fitz had no desire to argue. He knew he was right. He knew what he had smelled. He doubted he would ever forget it.

Then the medical worker touched a gloved hand to the outside of their helmet, nodding. Fitz guessed they were talking over comms, their external speaker off. Fitz turned to look back the way he'd just come from. Billows of black smoke mostly obscured the remains of the glider from his view, but as he kept his gaze fixed that way, he saw two figures climbing over the wreckage, forcing their way inside.

"We've got her," the medical worker said to him. Even through the distortion, Fitz could hear the sorrow in their voice.

"She's dead," Fitz said.

The medical worker nodded. "We're still getting her out of there. It will take a minute, but then we'll go. It's going to be hairy; this storm is going to make the shuttle flight back down to the landing field a real treat."

"Shuttle?" Fitz repeated. He saw no sign of one. He couldn't hear the roar of any engines nearby, not over the shrieking of the wind.

"It's up there," the medical worker said with a general wave of their hand. "No place to land. Where did you even set down?"

"Over that way," Fitz said.

"There's nothing over there," they said.

"You can't see it from here, but there's a meadow," Fitz said. He wished he didn't have to talk. He especially didn't want to have to talk about himself.

"Here they come," the medical worker said, and Fitz saw the other two emerging from the wisps of black smoke, a covered stretcher between them.

"Call down the shuttle," one of them said, voice just as genderless through the helmet as the first.

Fitz couldn't bear the sight of Jeger's body outlined under the flapping blanket. But even when he looked down at the toes of his own boots, he was aware of her presence there, so close.

Or rather, her lack of presence.

Had he done this? Had his maneuver caused this?

But how could it have? He came much closer to Ritchie's glider than he had to Jeger's. She had been fine. She had dodged his assault and recovered. She must have; never in a million years would Ritchie take a shot at a ship that was in an out-of-control tumble.

No, Jeger had been fine until Ritchie had shot her.

But the guns on their gliders weren't real. They weren't just for show; they were there to give the correct weight to the gliders for training purposes. But it wasn't possible to fire one. Even if someone put a live gun on a glider instead of a dummy one, the triggers in the yoke didn't connect to anything. He knew that for a fact. He had examined his glider far too closely on far too many occasions to not know for a certainty that that was true.

And yet, what had happened?

"Cadet," the first medical worker said, putting a hand on his shoulder. The gesture was muffled by the bulk of the glove. Fitz looked up to see a shuttle fighting to remain hovering over them as the winds tried to toss it about. There was no sign of the other two workers, or of Jeger. He guessed they were on the shuttle already. "We have to go."

Fitz got to his feet. He stood dumbly as the medical worker fastened a harness around him. He felt strangely distant, like he wasn't really there. He couldn't feel the wind he knew was freezing him. He couldn't feel the rock under his boots. The medical worker had to wrap Fitz's numb hands around the rope for him.

"Hold on tight. You'll be out of this in a second," they said. Fitz looked at his own hands, which seemed incapable of following that command. Slowly, as if his flesh had been turned to something only a little more flexible than stone, he curled his fingers until they managed a grip of sorts.

Then he was rocketing up into the sky, the medical worker close beside him. Despite the speed of their ascent, the worker kept an arm out to hover a hand near Fitz's elbow, just in case he needed any assistance.

A flurry of hands came out of the shuttle, grabbing his flight suit to haul him inside, out of the wind. Once he was inside, and they had dragged him to the middle of the space between open doorways, the medical worker pulled themself inside and flopped down on the ground next to Fitz.

Then the doors closed, and the shriek of the wind was gone. There was nothing but blissful silence.

Fitz looked up and saw Jeger's covered body on the floor of the shuttle, no more than a meter away from his own toes. He tucked his feet a little closer in.

"Whew," the medical worker said, and Fitz realized the helmet distortion was gone from their voice. It was definitely a man, but a young one, not much older than he was. The man rubbed at his sweaty forehead, then finally sat up, scooting across the shuttle floor on his butt until he reached one of the windows. "Hey, I see your glider down there. If it survives the storm, we'll have to retrieve it later."

Then he crawled back to Fitz's side, but Fitz kept his eyes carefully on his own knees.

"That was a hell of a landing, cadet," the man said. "That meadow is barely bigger than the size of your craft, and you did that in a glider? You must be one hell of a pilot."

Fitz lifted his eyes and fixed them on the medical worker. He watched as the adrenaline-high ebullience faded from that man's face. Only when the last of it was gone, and the man was appropriately sober, did Fitz drop his eyes back to his knees.

There was a little speck of gravel from the mountainside, still on the knee of his flight suit. He kept all of his attention focused on that. But even without looking at it, he couldn't shut out the memory of the brief glimpse he'd gotten of Jeger's grayish hand laying curled up on the floor, just peeking out from under the covering blanket.

7

RITCHIE TOOK her helmet off as her glider rode the elevator down to the hangar floor. People were still chattering away, but she couldn't get her mind to focus hard enough to catch any actual words.

But they were upset. She could tell they were upset. Frightened and anxious.

But all Ritchie felt was numb. What had just happened?

The towing system parked her glider in its slot, and she lifted the cockpit door to climb out. A crowd was already waiting for her to reach the ground, and more cadets were running from the other end of the room.

They were still all talking at once, and her brain was leaving it at a wall of noise. Like she wasn't ready to confront actual words yet.

Then someone was shaking her, hard enough to make her teeth clack against each other. She reflexively brought up her arms to break the hold before realizing it was Cadet Captain Bale.

"Ritchie?!?" His voice was pleading for her to answer a question she hadn't heard at all.

"What happened?" Ritchie asked. "Did Jeger crash?"

"You don't know?" Bale said incredulously. "But you were the one that was there."

"I didn't see," Ritchie said. The crowd around her had quieted to just whispered exchanges amongst themselves. Ritchie looked from face to face, various degrees of shock and grief looking back out at her. "Where's Fitz?"

"Fitz?" Bale asked, also looking around.

"He landed up there on the mountain," Moreau said, and Ritchie realized she was standing just at Ritchie's elbow. Had she been there the whole time?

"He crashed?" Bale asked.

"No, landed," Moreau said.

"I've flown around that peak a thousand times. There's no place to land a glider up there," Bale said.

Moreau just shrugged.

"Which mountain?" Ritchie asked.

"The one Jeger crashed into," Moreau said.

"What could you see?" Ritchie asked.

"And how could you see it?" Bale asked. "You were already landed, same as the rest of us."

"To answer the second question first," Moreau said, turning to face Bale, "I hacked into the drone feeds of those two novice cadets. You knew the ones; they're always watching from the edge of the field when we drill combat maneuvers. They must be cutting class to be out there; maybe you should look into that."

"Were you doing this during the exercise?" Bale asked.

"Are you crazy? I have too much information to sort through as it is. I'm a *terrible* pilot," Moreau said, and it almost sounded like she was bragging. "I was one of the first shot down. I usually am. But it's maddening waiting on the others, and the glider systems only give you access to the comms, which don't exactly paint a picture. But those kids, Keller and Wyss, they're always out there. I asked them once what they were up to, and they said they were gathering data. They track relative positions and velocities or something. I think that Wyss kid is trying to create a flight tactics algorithm? At any rate, they gave me access to their visual feeds last semester. I can log in after I land and watch them live through my visor display."

"So when you say hacked..." Bale prompted.

"Well, Wyss hacked it," Moreau said. "Or changed the programming or whatever. The point is, I could see everything."

"I couldn't," Ritchie said. "I saw I got the hit, and I guess I celebrated a little. I couldn't see Jeger's glider, but that's always true after you get a hit. I didn't know anything was wrong until I started to hear the chatter over the comms. I took off my visor and could see Jeger's glider. It looked like it was going to crash. But then my own glider landed, and I couldn't see a thing. She crashed, didn't she?"

"She did," Bale said. "The emergency medical team that was standing by scrambled out on a shuttle right away, but I haven't heard anything yet. I haven't heard from Fitz yet either. Stars, I hope there weren't *two* crashes."

"Jeger crashed because her glider was damaged," Moreau said. "It was missing most of one wing."

"What?" Ritchie and Bale said at once.

"I know it sounds crazy and impossible. It should be impossible, right?" Moreau said, glancing at Ritchie uncomfortably, then away again. "But I guess Keller and Wyss have tons of proof of what I saw."

"What did you see?" Bale said, taking a step closer to loom over her. Moreau was the shortest of the cadets—Ritchie suspected strings had been pulled to add a few centimeters to her official height so she could just squeak by the requirements to get in at the academy—but she was unbothered by Bale's attempts at intimidation. She just looked up at him calmly.

"Ritchie didn't just nail that shot in the simulation," Moreau said. "She shot Jeger for real. When she pulled the trigger, the gun actually fired. Her laser took out Jeger's wing, and it was all over. There was no way she could get her glider under control to get it back to the landing field, and she was too close to the ground for the emergency team to get to her in time."

"No," Ritchie said. "No, that can't be."

"Jeger wasn't her first kill," Bale said, then flinched at his own word choice. "I mean, Ritchie took out six other gliders on Jeger's team. None of those resulted in her gun actually firing."

Moreau shrugged. "I don't know how it happened; I just know it did. Maybe Fitz saw more; he was pretty close. Or Keller and Wyss have more data that tells a fuller story."

"Where is Fitz?" Ritchie asked.

"Like I said, he landed," Moreau said. "He set down on an open meadow no bigger than the glider elevator over there. I don't know how he planned to get down from there without his glider. Walk?"

"The responders will get him," Bale said. "I should make sure they know about him, though." He gave Ritchie's shoulder one last squeeze, then jogged across the hangar to the command room.

Ritchie was relieved to see that the crowd had mostly broken up into smaller groups, all talking amongst themselves. She was no longer the focus of dozens of pairs of eyes.

She turned to Moreau. "You could've told that story a little better," she said. "You made it sound like I shot Jeger."

"You *did* shoot Jeger," Moreau said.

"I had no idea the gun was live," Ritchie said.

"I never said you did it on purpose," Moreau said.

"You could've—" Ritchie started to say, but then stopped as she heard boots pounding as someone marched angrily across the hangar deck. She could see a disturbance where a few of the groups of whispering cadets would look up, then quickly get out of the way of whoever was coming.

It was Cadet Egli. She looked terrible. Her face was puffy and tear-streaked, and her hair was coming out of its tight updo. But she kept on marching, not needing to push cadets aside but clearly willing to do so, until she was toe to toe with Ritchie.

Ritchie fought the urge to shrink under the angry intensity of Egli's eyes.

"You did this!" Egli said, pounding a finger into Ritchie's chest. Moreau started forward, fists coming up, but Ritchie put out a hand to stop her.

"It's all a mistake," Ritchie said. "But we can get to the bottom of it. The flight recorders and—"

"You did this!" Egli said again, louder this time. The finger jabbing into Ritchie's sternum was starting to hurt. "You killed her!"

"She's dead?" Ritchie asked.

"We don't know that yet," Moreau said. "The crash looked bad, but the gliders are designed to protect the pilot. There's even reason to think—"

"She's dead!" Egli all but shrieked. "They're bringing her body down now!"

Ritchie felt sick. She hadn't even eaten any breakfast, but her stomach was still threatening to force up what bitter bile it contained. She could taste it on the back of her tongue.

"Ritchie didn't do this," Moreau said with total confidence. She put an arm around Ritchie's shoulders. Ritchie was still trying not to vomit. Or to meet Egli's eyes again. "Something went very wrong, but it wasn't Ritchie's fault."

"Who else would do this?" Egli asked with a humorless laugh. "Who else? Who else had a reason to?"

At that, Ritchie forced her spine to straighten. She lifted her chin and sort of met Egli's eyes. "That's not true. I had no reason to ever hurt Jeger."

"Come on!" Egli said, throwing up her hands then turning to make eye contact with the intensely uncomfortable cadets who still lingered nearby. "Who here believes that's true? Any of you? Anyone?"

"You have no proof of motive," Moreau said, and Ritchie grit her teeth again. Was there any way she could get Moreau *not* to defend her?

"Everyone knows that Ritchie here has a deep hatred of Jeger," Egli said. Then her voice choked as she corrected, "had."

"I never hated her," Ritchie said, but her words were little more than a whisper. Her throat was starting to close up on her.

"We all know you did," Egli said, brushing away fresh tears with the back of her hand. "She gave you a hard time, but she had to. You weren't remotely prepared for this place. And we all saw the look in your eyes every time she busted you. That angry determination. We all knew you were swearing that one day you'd get her back. Well, I guess you did."

"I never..." Ritchie said, but the tightening in her throat was just too much for her to go on. She looked past Egli to the other cadets. Did they all think the same thing? That every time Ritchie had been determined to she would show she was better the next time, to take her punishment and grow stronger for it, to not let Jeger get to her, had they all thought that was her swearing violent revenge?

But none of them would meet her gaze.

"We shouldn't be discussing this," Moreau said, stepping away from Ritchie to catch hold of Egli's arm. "There will be an investigation. Testimonials, maybe. But they'll happen when everyone's blood is a little colder. This just now isn't helpful."

"She did it," Egli said again, but this time her angry swiping at her face couldn't touch all the tears. Moreau murmured something that Ritchie couldn't hear, then looked over Egli's shoulder into the crowd.

Grof and Frei were there, and when Moreau looked their way, they came forward to put their arms around Egli.

"Should we take her back to the barracks?" Grof asked Moreau.

"Just the command room for now, I think," Moreau said. "Until we get orders, we should all stay here. There might be questioning."

Ritchie put a hand over her mouth and turned away from the others, but instantly regretted that movement when her eyes fell on the gun under the nose of her glider. The gun that had betrayed her.

What had happened? She started walking towards it, reaching out a hand to touch it. Was it still warm? Was there something obviously wrong about it, something she missed on her preflight? Something she should've noticed?

"Don't," Moreau said, catching hold of Ritchie just before her fingertips could brush over the gleaming barrel. "Don't touch it."

"But we have to figure out what happened," Ritchie said.

"That's not on us," Moreau said. "I know why you want to. I want to know what happened too. And I believe you when you say you didn't know there was anything wrong with it."

"But what if I made a mistake?" Ritchie asked.

"Then we'll deal with that when we know what the mistake was," Moreau said. "But for now, we have to leave this for the official investigation." She leaned closer to whisper in Ritchie's ear, "I don't think anyone here is going to back up Egli's theory on your motive, okay?

You're not the only one who's been given a hard time by Jeger. But if you do anything that looks like tampering with evidence—"

"Got it," Ritchie said. "Yes, you're right." She straightened up and stepped away from the glider, keeping her hands clearly in view in case anyone was watching.

Then they all heard the sound of one of the shuttle elevators running and turned to see the emergency medical team's shuttle moving down towards the hangar deck. Moreau caught Ritchie's hand and gave it a squeeze before they joined the others in gathering close around the shuttle's lowering ramp.

"Oh," one of the medical team said when he poked his head out and saw them all waiting below. "Step back and make a hole. We've got a fallen cadet coming through."

Despite the voice in Ritchie's head admonishing her not to chase false hope, her heart clung to the flimsy chance that "fallen" here just meant "injured."

But then the stretcher started slowly hovering down the ramp, and she could see that the entire body was covered in a dark blanket. No one spoke a word as they watched it pass down the center of the hangar deck towards the command room, but Ritchie could hear sniffles and muffled sobs. Jeger might not have been well-liked, but no one had ever wanted to see her like this.

Except, clearly, someone had. Because Ritchie's gut wasn't saying "mistake." It was saying "sabotage." But was the culprit hoping to kill Jeger, or frame Ritchie, or both?

When the stretcher was out of sight, Ritchie once more felt the weight of too many pairs of eyes on her. Did they think she was guilty? Did people actually believe she could do this? After knowing her for an entire semester, is this really what they thought of her?

"Cadet Ritchie."

Ritchie looked up to see Hansen standing over her.

"Oh, Colonel Hansen," she cried, for a single moment feeling actual relief to see him there. Like he was there to fix everything.

Then she saw the security team behind him.

"What's going on?" Moreau asked, moving to stand between Ritchie and Hansen.

"This is just a precautionary measure," Hansen said. "Until we know what happened."

"You're arresting her?" Moreau said. "Just her?"

"She was the one who fired a live weapon," someone in the crowd said. Ritchie looked around but couldn't tell who had spoken those words.

"She is being detained," Hansen said.

"How's that different?" Moreau demanded.

"Moreau, it's all right," Ritchie said. At the moment, an armed guard to escort her off the hangar deck was feeling rather welcome. "I'll go quietly."

Hansen raised a single brow as if finding the idea of her not going quietly mildly amusing.

Then the security officer to his left stepped forward and snapped restraints around Ritchie's wrists. She hadn't expected to be cuffed, but it was over before she could even summon a protest. Then two of them caught hold of her elbows and started to march her towards the command room.

"Ritchie?" Moreau asked, pushing cadets out of her way in her attempt to keep alongside her buddy.

"You stay here, cadet," Hansen commanded her.

"But—"

"Cadet!" Hansen bellowed. "You've been given an order."

Moreau gave Ritchie one last look, then fell back.

When they were at the command room door, Ritchie looked back over her shoulder as if she wanted to see the hangar deck one last time.

Had she left all this behind forever? Would she ever get a chance to fly again? Or would she be dismissed from the academy and sent back home?

Or worse, would she end up in detention like Weld, the crazy recruit that had tried to kill her on the train ride to the school?

Despair threatened to overwhelm her, but then she saw a flicker of motion on the shuttle ramp. One last emergency medical team member leaving the shuttle?

No. She would know that dark hair anywhere, at any distance. It was Fitz. He was okay. He had made it down off the mountain.

He stopped halfway down the ramp when he was still a little higher up than the other cadets and scanned the crowd, then the rows of gliders. But before he had worked his way far enough back to see her, she was being pulled along again, through the door and into the command room, where more officers awaited her.

So many officers.

8

IT WAS like any functioning part of Fitz's brain had just switched off. The entire shuttle ride he had just stared fixedly at his own knees but couldn't stop his mind from seeing Jeger's exposed hand. He was vaguely aware of murmurs, the three emergency medical team members around him speaking to each other, or perhaps to him. He didn't bother to listen, so he didn't really know.

Then the shuttle landed, and two of the medics took Jeger's body away. The third bustled around the shuttle interior, stowing equipment and starting the decontamination drones working. Only after those drones were airborne, spraying down the cockpit interior, did the medic come back to rest a hand on Fitz's shoulder.

"Time to go," he said softly.

Fitz looked up at him mutely, but then pushed himself up to his feet and headed for the ramp to the hangar deck. He could hear voices below, cadets talking together. The rise and fall of their voices spoke of some sort of excitement, but not in a good way. Agitated anxiety, maybe.

Then he was far enough down the ramp to see them gathered there. They were standing in groups mostly, but he saw Moreau standing alone. She was apart from the others, closer to the central area of the hangar deck, but her back was to him.

He looked around for Ritchie, scanning the crowd, then looking towards where her glider was docked. But there was no sign of her.

Just what was Moreau looking at? He followed the direction of her gaze to the door to the command center. But it was closed, the usually transparent window between the deck and that room now opaque.

"I have to seal this up," the medic said, and Fitz realized he was waiting for Fitz to finish going down the ramp.

"Sorry," Fitz mumbled, getting out of the way, then continuing on to Moreau's side. "What's going on?" he asked her.

Moreau looked over at him with worried eyes. "They've arrested Ritchie."

Just like that, the numb, detached feeling was gone. Fitz seldom got angry, but the liquid warmth suddenly rushing through him was a pretty close approximation to that feeling.

"Arrested her? But why? They can't have even tried to figure out what happened yet," Fitz said.

"Maybe 'detained' is a better word," Moreau said. "I don't know what they're doing. I have to find Keller and Wyss."

"They're novice cadets; why would they be here?" Fitz asked, but she was already gone.

Fitz looked around at the other cadets, but no one was meeting his eyes. Was that because they knew Ritchie was his friend or because they thought he might be guilty of murder?

Both, he decided. Thrusting his hands deep in his pockets, he marched off the deck and up into the pelting rain. He didn't quicken his steps across the open field, and by the time he reached the library doors, he was thoroughly soaked.

The outer doors closed behind him, but the inner doors remained shut. A pair of blowers dropped down from the ceiling and hit him with a blast of hot air, rotating around him until he was thoroughly dry. His uniform was made of a quick-drying material, so this didn't take long. And after a semester on Oymyakon, he was used to it.

Then the inner doors opened, and he stepped into the library. At first, he was surprised to hear the soft murmur of voices and realize that cadets were all around him, chatting together or studying, just like any other day.

But then only his class had combat flight today. No one else knew yet what had happened.

Fitz kept walking, hands in his pockets forming fists. He wanted to storm into some place, to do something explosive, but he didn't know what.

He knew what he'd do if he were in Ritchie's place. He had been detained on more than one occasion in the past, occasionally for things he hadn't done, but mostly for things he had. He knew whom he would demand to speak to, and what he would say.

But he had never been in this situation before, wanting to speak on someone else's behalf. He wasn't sure how to begin.

Then he realized with a start that his feet had carried him through the library, then turned to take him down the long hallway of the administrative wing. Well, part of him had an idea where to start, anyway. He continued on until he reached Colonel Hansen's office. He knocked briskly, but opened the door without waiting for an answer. He took a deep breath, prepared to say everything on his mind so quickly and so loudly that Hansen would have no opportunity to interrupt.

But the office was empty.

Fitz consulted his implant and verified from the academy schedules that Hansen wasn't supposed to be teaching at that hour. No one had booked his time for any other purpose. So, where was he? Running in the gym? Still in his bunk?

Fitz slammed the door as he left the office. It had probably been a waste of time, anyway.

When Fitz emerged back into the main hallway, he saw it was filled with cadets from his class. Someone must have told them all to evacuate the hangar deck. But none of them were heading to their next classes. It was too early for that, anyway. The combat flight exercise should've been followed by a long debrief where all of their actions were replayed and critiqued by Jeger and Bale. Clearly, that had been canceled.

Most of the cadets were gathering at tables in the cafeteria. Fitz stood uncertainly near the doorway, looking for anyone he knew. He saw his roommates, Imhof and Stucki, at a table together and headed that way. The two cadets were speaking to each other in furious whispers, heads close together over the center of the table, so Fitz was nearly on top of them before he could hear their words.

"Of course she did something," Imhof was saying, tapping a finger on the tabletop in emphasis. "Of course she did. What else could've happened?" Fitz froze in his steps, unseen by either of them, although all they had to do was glance up from the table.

"I don't know that we know what *did* happen," Stucki said.

"I told you, she fired a live laser cannon," Imhof said.

"Man, this is no time for spreading rumors," Stucki said, shaking his head sorrowfully.

"It's true," Imhof insisted.

"I don't know," Stucki said, still shaking his head. "I think we should wait until command announces something. We don't know anything until then."

"We know she doesn't belong here," Imhof said.

"She belongs here," Fitz said. They both looked up at him at once. Stucki's cheeks flamed red, but Imhof only scowled.

"Eavesdropping, Fitz?" he asked.

Fitz shrugged.

"Weren't you up there, man?" Stucki asked. Fitz nodded. "Did you see anything?"

"Jeger's glider had lost a wing," Fitz said. "I didn't see how that happened."

"Live laser cannon fire," Imhof said firmly.

"Okay," Fitz said. "I did hear what sounded like live fire. But from where? Nothing else was up there."

Imhof rolled his eyes. "From Ritchie's glider, of course."

"But that makes no sense," Fitz said.

"Well, if it had been from your glider, I imagine you'd be the one wearing cuffs now," Imhof said.

"They took Ritchie away in *cuffs*?" Fitz said, then shook his head to clear the distressing image of that. "But no. There's no way our gliders can shoot actual lasers. They've been disabled, and even if they functioned, they're not wired into the cockpit."

"Not normally, no," Stucki said.

"You think Ritchie found a workaround?" Fitz demanded.

"Not me," Stucki said, raising his hands in surrender. "Man, I don't even want to be talking about this. Not when we don't have any facts at all."

"Jeger is dead," Imhof said. "There's a fact for you."

"Ritchie would never do that," Fitz said.

"But she could, right?" Imhof said, leaning in conspiratorially. "If she wanted to, she could figure out a way to do it. We've all seen how clever she is."

"First, she doesn't belong here, and now she's diabolically clever?" Fitz said. "When I said she would never do that, I meant it. She would never *choose* to do such a thing. Whether or not she was mentally capable of it isn't the question. Morally, she'd never do it."

"I guess we'll find out what she is capable of morally when they interrogate her," Imhof said. "I think like Stucki I'm going to wait for better information. No offense, but you being her bestie doesn't exactly lead me to want to take your word as to her character."

"Leave me out of it, man," Stucki said, pushing back from the table.

"What do you know about Ritchie's moral character, anyway?" Fitz grumbled. Mostly to himself, because he was ready to push back from this conversation as well. But not entirely to himself, because a part of him really wanted to get into it with Imhof.

But that wasn't going to help anyone.

"I know what we all know," Imhof said, waving his hands at the other cadets around the room. "She drove that recruit mad, the one on the train. She drove him into a homicidal rage."

"What?" Fitz sputtered. "Who's been saying that? Because the only other people on that train who are here now are me, Moreau, and Hansen. And I know for a fact none of the three of us have been saying anything remotely like that."

"I told you that was just a rumor, man," Stucki hissed at Imhof.

"There's clearly something off about her, you have to admit it," Imhof said to Stucki. "She's so quiet, keeping to herself, never bonding with anyone but apparently her train mates. She misses a question in class, and the next day she's a master of the topic. Who does that?"

"Someone who's really trying to belong here," Fitz said. "Forget it," he added, throwing up a hand to stop whatever onslaught of words Imhof wanted to retort with. "Just forget I ever said anything. Have either of you seen Moreau?"

"No, sorry," Stucki said.

"You mean your other train mate?" Imhof asked. "Is she in on it, too?"

"I'm not even going to ask what that means," Fitz said and turned away.

"Because you know what it means!" Imhof said. There was a clatter of a chair falling over, and Fitz guessed that Imhof was now on his feet, yelling at Fitz's back, maybe making some exuberant gestures. He wasn't going to turn around to see, that was for sure.

But Imhof kept yelling anyway, and Fitz was all too aware of every other conversation stopping, of all the other cadets now looking Fitz's way.

"It means the two of you were clearly in cahoots!" Imhof yelled. "It was only the two of you up there with Jeger, there at the end. And *you* weren't even supposed to be up there! I think Ritchie killed her, but I also think you were in on it. Maybe your friend Moreau, too. The truth is going to come out one way or the other!"

Fitz just kept walking. At the doorway, he raised a hand to wave back over his shoulder, just a casual little flutter.

Then he started walking double-time back towards the library. He had to find Moreau. He was suddenly very curious what she had meant when she said she had to find Keller and Wyss.

What did those two kids have to do with anything?

                                     9

RITCHIE SAT ALONE in the brig, staring at her hands and going over in her head everything she had said in the command room. She had told them everything that had happened, everything she had done, from the moment she first touched her glider that morning to the moment she was arrested.

Detained, she corrected herself. That's what they kept telling her. She was *detained.*

As if the word made any difference. About the third time through answering the same questions, she had realized they were trying to trip her up. They were waiting for her to say something that contradicted something else she said earlier. Which had made her super paranoid. She hadn't done anything wrong, and she had answered every question truthfully. But she was afraid that somewhere in there she had said something just a little bit wrong. They phrased the questions so carefully. So trickily.

And just when she thought it was all over, they started again from the beginning.

But eventually, they had run out of questions to ask. Then she had been taken to a detention cell.

She hadn't even realized there were detention cells. She knew that ships had them, but she didn't think a school would. Not even a foreign service academy.

It didn't look like what she thought a detention cell would look like, but she had to admit she had only ever seen them in videos, never in real life. She had expected something cold and bare with no amenities. So she was a bit surprised to see herself being led into a rather nice barracks room.

It was the same size as the one she shared with Moreau, Grof, and Frei, although this one had only the single set of bunk beds. Where the other set would be stood a door into a private bath with shower. There was even still a desk at the foot of the bed and a locker beside it.

After the guards had shut the door and left her there, she had opened the locker to find a spare blanket resting inside it, but nothing else. The desk's surface lit up like a normal one did, but required a passcode to access any of the academy's systems.

Perhaps they'd give her one later so she could keep up with the work from the classes she was already missing. If they *detained* her for more than a few hours.

Ritchie dropped her head into her hands in despair. She had answered so many questions, but no one would answer a single one of hers.

She didn't understand what had happened, or how. And no one would answer when she asked what was being done to investigate. Someone had done something to the gun on her glider, but who? Why? And when?

Occasionally the whirlpool of her rushing thoughts would quiet to something like an exhausted stillness. In those moments, the same thought kept rising up to the surface.

Who had Egli been talking to Jeger about? Who was that "him?"

And then she'd feel a flush of shame. For reasons she avoided articulating to herself, she had never mentioned what she had overheard in the showers that morning. She could mount a pretty good defense that it didn't seem relevant. She never for one minute thought that Egli had anything to do with what had happened to Jeger.

And yet, her gut was telling her there was something there. Something she had to follow up on.

But she couldn't. Not from the detention cell.

She was still chasing her own thoughts around aimlessly when the door clanked open again, and the guards came in to lift her off the bunk by her elbows.

Calling them guards might be overstating it; they were cadets just like she was whose work detail this week was guard duty. Next week they'd be in the kitchens washing pots and pans.

At least they didn't cuff her this time.

She walked between them as they guided her down the hall to another door, where they stopped. One of the guards knocked, and after a pause, the door opened. But when they stepped inside, there was no one there. Some sort of automation, Ritchie guessed.

They led Ritchie inside and pushed her towards a chair on one side of a long, narrow table. Ritchie sat down on the hard, cold plastic.

"Cuffs?" one of the guards asked the other.

"No one said to cuff her," the other said.

"They didn't say *not* to cuff her," the first one said.

The other one sighed, then looked down at Ritchie. "Why don't you just keep your hands on the table in full view, okay?"

"Like this?" Ritchie asked, putting her palms on the even colder metal surface of the table and spreading her fingers wide.

"Perfect," he said. "We've never dealt with a murder charge before," he added.

"So no one thinks this might have just been an accident?" she asked, feeling the last of her hope evaporating away.

The two guards traded a glance but said nothing.

"Wait here. Someone will be in in a moment," the first guard said. "We'll be just outside the door."

"I'm not planning on going anywhere," Ritchie said.

This time, she was only alone for a moment. Then the door opened again, and a cadet she didn't recognize came into the room with three steaming drinks in a tray. He set one in front of Ritchie, then set the other two on the other side of the table. He then headed back towards the door but had to step aside, holding the tray close to his chest, as two more people came in from the hallway.

The first was Cadet Captain Bale. The other was Colonel Hansen.

"What's going on?" Ritchie asked, as Bale took the first seat across from her and set a tablet down in front of him.

"We just have a few questions," Colonel Hansen said, settling in beside Bale as the guards in the hallway pulled the door shut with a resounding clang.

"Haven't I already answered all the questions?" Ritchie asked tiredly.

"From command, yes," Colonel Hansen said. He had been in that room the entire time, but he had never asked her a thing. He had only stood near the door, arms folded and head bowed, listening. "There's been some debate about how we should approach this."

"You mean like as an accident or as a crime?" Ritchie asked hopefully.

"No," Hansen said. "I'm afraid there's no possibility that it wasn't a crime."

"Oh," Ritchie said and looked down at her own hands.

"That tea is for you," Hansen said, perhaps thinking she was eying the cup. Ritchie seized it, but only to wrap her hands around its warmth. She didn't take a drink.

"The debate is whether the seriousness of the charge negates the usual protocol," Bale said, and Ritchie turned her attention to him.

He looked wrecked. Like he'd gone for days without sleep, and yet it wasn't even noon yet. He rubbed at his reddened eyes as he consulted something on his tablet screen.

"I don't understand," Ritchie said.

"Usual protocol is for the cadet captains to handle these things, conduct an investigation and make disciplinary recommendations to command," Hansen said.

"But there's just Bale now," Ritchie said.

"Cadet Captain Bale," Hansen gently corrected her. "And you are correct. But it's been decided to follow the standard protocol even in this case. Cadet Captain Bale will be relying on the cadet lieutenants for assistance as needed."

"But Jeger is dead," Ritchie said, and she could hear her voice catch. "This isn't a game."

"Do you think anything we do here is a game, cadet?" Hansen asked coldly.

"No, sir," Ritchie said.

"I was there when you were questioned this morning," Bale said, his eyes still on his tablet. "And I took notes. So we shouldn't have to go back over any of that again."

"Thank you," Ritchie said. Then, just to have something to do, she took a sip from the tea. It was light, sweet and refreshing, and it made her want to cry. Shouldn't they be serving her bitter, over-steeped dreck? If they thought she was guilty?

"Okay," Bale said, still scanning whatever was on his tablet screen. Hansen sat back in his chair and folded his hands on the table, but said nothing. "All right," Bale said and looked up at Ritchie. "I guess my first question would be, do you know of any evidence that could clear you of suspicion?"

Hansen raised his eyebrows but remained silent.

"Oh," Ritchie said, completely caught off guard. "I don't think so. Not one thing. Like the opposite of a smoking gun? Nothing like that."

"No, I didn't expect so," Bale said, scanning his notes again.

"Isn't the burden of proof the other way around?" Ritchie asked.

"Oh, yeah," Bale said, nodding. "I just meant, if you could prove you didn't do it, that would change things a lot."

"But someone is doing a proper investigation already, right?" Ritchie asked, looking from Bale to the silent Hansen and then back again.

"Of course," Bale said. "There is a team on the hangar deck now tearing your glider and its laser cannon apart and cataloging the evidence."

"Because I didn't tamper with my glider's armaments," Ritchie said. She tried taking another drink of tea to calm down, but it didn't help. She just wiped her lips afterward and kept going. "Hangar deck surveillance videos. Was anyone in the area of my glider who shouldn't be? I've been flying that glider daily throughout the inter-semester breaks. That's a lot of preflight checklists. Those have to be evidence, too, right? Some of them were double-checked by the colonel."

Bale glanced over at Hansen, who gave a small nod to indicate he had indeed double-checked her work.

"Someone tampered with both my gun and my firing system inside the cockpit. They must have left evidence. Fingerprints or something," Ritchie said.

"It's all being looked into," Hansen assured her.

"And?"

"So far, I've heard nothing," he said. "But the team has orders to contact me the minute they discover anything."

"And then you'll tell me?" Ritchie asked.

"That will really depend on what they find, I'm afraid," Hansen said.

"And Keller and Wyss? Their drones?"

"There's a team on that as well. Again, nothing so far," Hansen said.

"It's only been an hour or two," Bale said to her.

Ritchie nodded, not trusting herself to speak.

"Anything else, cadet captain?" Hansen asked.

"Well, this is maybe a bit of a long shot," Bale said, glancing at Hansen before turning his attention back to Ritchie. "And obviously anything you'd say would have to be confirmed before we even followed up on it, I should think."

Hansen's brow was up again, but he didn't intervene.

"What is it?" Ritchie asked.

"Look, you and I both know that Jeger wasn't exactly popular with the other cadets," Bale said.

"Okay," Ritchie said slowly.

"Yeah," Bale said. "The thing is, I have a pretty good idea from my side of things who has said what in the past. I have a few cadets I'm going to be talking to among my own squad later today. Just to see what they have to say, right?"

"What are you asking me?" Ritchie asked.

"I know you've only been here a semester, but that's probably long enough, right? To get to know the other cadets on your side of the barracks?"

"A bit," Ritchie said.

"And some of them maybe have had things to say about Jeger in the past? Especially to you, who was, let's face it, her favorite victim."

"I was never a victim," Ritchie said sharply.

"Er, no. Sorry. Badly worded," Bale said.

"Are you asking the cadet to provide you with grist for your rumor mill, cadet captain?" Hansen asked with a dangerous edge to his voice.

"Absolutely not," Bale said, putting up both his hands as if to ward off any such grist. "I'm just saying, I have to start talking to other people. For background, right? And I'm asking Cadet Ritchie if she has any place in particular where she thinks I should start."

Hansen looked like he was about to say something, but then changed his mind. He stroked at his chin for a moment, then stopped to take a drink of his tea.

Ritchie shuddered at the memory of just how he liked his tea. Smoky to the point of tasting ashy, and far too sweet. Ugh.

Then Hansen set his cup back down and looked at Ritchie. "I think I'll allow this question. Do you have an answer, Cadet Ritchie?"

Ritchie looked down at her hands squeezing together around the now-empty tea mug. She could think of ten names easy of other cadets who had expressed some pretty strong dislike to Jeger. Maybe twenty more who had been a little less vehement in their feelings, but those feelings had still been negative. Some of those cadets had approached Ritchie out of sympathy, having been the butt of Jeger's training methods before. Some had come out the other end of it with no sympathy for others at all; if they had gone through it, so should everyone else.

But Ritchie no more believed any of them were actually capable of murder than she believed herself was. And why would they act now, anyway? Since Ritchie had come to the academy, everyone else largely escaped Jeger's attentions. No one else's performance could ever look as bad as Ritchie's as she struggled to catch up to the rest of the class.

The memory floated up again, of Egli and Jeger arguing in the showers. But that hadn't been murderous rage either. Something had been going on, but was it more than the usual cadet drama?

She couldn't really know. Not without knowing who the "him" was and what had happened.

"No," Ritchie said at last. "I can't think of anyone."

Bale looked disappointed as he switched off his tablet and tucked it away. But she could swear Hansen had picked up his mug and drank the last of its contents to hide his own look of... was it satisfaction?

Clearly, Ritchie had just been tested without even realizing it. She was just grateful that it seemed like she had passed.

10

AFTER CHECKING every window alcove and all along the central studying table, Fitz still hadn't found Moreau. Had she gone down to the barracks? He wasn't supposed to go down the hallway to that side of the barracks, but it wasn't like he'd never broken a rule before. He had a half dozen excuses for doing just that which had worked well in the past.

Then he saw one of the meeting rooms had its glass walls set to opaque.

Statistically, how likely was she to be in there? Fitz was pretty sure that percentage chance varied widely between what was true if he knocked to check and what would be true if he decided to try the barracks first. That made little sense logically, but Fitz tended to trust his gut over logic. It generally served him well.

He knocked on the door. He could hear a murmur of voices inside, but even when he pressed his face to the glass and cupped his hands around his eyes, he couldn't see through the window. He knocked again, more loudly.

"Moreau?" he called. If she wasn't in there, whoever was could just yell at him to go away.

The door swung open, and the room within was all darkness. Then

Moreau stuck her head out, blinking in the comparatively bright light of the library.

"Fitz," she said. "Come in."

She ducked back in the room, pushing the door wider open behind her so he could follow. He had a brief glimpse of two faces leaning over the central holographic table before the door clicked shut behind him, and they were back in darkness.

"What's going on here?" he asked. "Was that Wyss and Keller I saw in here with you?"

"Yeah," Moreau said in a whisper. "They're going over the footage from their drone swarm."

"What drone swarm?" he asked, also in a whisper. Apparently, whatever Wyss and Keller were working on needed quiet.

"Oh yeah, you weren't there when I explained all this before to Ritchie," Moreau said.

"How is Ritchie?" Fitz asked.

"One question at a time, okay?" Moreau said. "Second question first: I haven't seen her since the last time I saw you. But before that, she was doing about as well as can be expected since she thinks this is all her fault somehow."

"What? She doesn't think *she* murdered Jeger?"

"Quiet or go outside," Keller said from out of the darkness. Now that his eyes had adjusted, Fitz could just make out the lines of her face outlined by the display she was leaning over.

"Sorry," Fitz said to her, then whispered to Moreau, "but she doesn't, does she?"

"Obviously it was an accident," Moreau said. "She didn't mean for that gun to fire; she had no idea that it would. But she thinks she missed something that she should've caught."

"But I don't think it was an accident," Fitz said. "That's not possible. Somebody tampered with something. That's not Ritchie's fault."

"But even if that's true, Ritchie thinks she should've noticed that tampering," Moreau said with a shrug. "You know how she is."

"I know how she is," Fitz agreed. "She's probably going nuts now. I'm sure she's dying to investigate all this herself, but can't since she's locked up in detention. For no reason; how could anyone think she did this?"

"Well, we're trying to see if we can give command enough of a reasonable doubt to at least let her go while the investigation is ongoing," Moreau said. "I gather they're just worried that the other cadets blame her. They don't need to hold her in detention to keep her from leaving the planet, right? So if we can just find something that will shift suspicion away from her in the eyes of the other cadets, they might let her out. Which is what I'm hoping, anyway. She's going to explode if she misses any more classes."

Fitz gave a short laugh, partly because he could picture just that, but partly because he and Moreau were about to miss a class of their own in a few minutes.

"Okay, drone swarm?" he said.

"That's a project Keller and I have been working on," Wyss said. He'd gotten up from his chair and was standing at Fitz's elbow. And not much higher. The kid was nearly as short as Moreau.

"What sort of project?" Fitz asked.

"We've been deploying swarms of drones to observe all the flight exercises, although we've been paying particular attention to the combat flight exercises," Wyss said.

"'Paying particular attention to' is a phrase which here means that they've been cutting classes to watch our classes live," Moreau said.

"It's important," Wyss said. "If our algorithm works, we can really refine the way everyone approaches strategy and tactics."

"So, this isn't an official class assignment?" Fitz guessed.

Keller snorted. "Like class assignments are anything like this challenging."

"They're going over all the footage and data now, looking for clues," Moreau said.

"Have you found anything?" he asked, afraid to let that spark of hope in his chest grow.

"Nothing good," Moreau said. "We have footage of Ritchie blowing Jeger out of the sky, then punching her fists in the air in celebration from like a thousand angles."

"And in that footage, her visor is down?" Fitz said.

"Yeah, so she had no idea," Moreau said. "But that's not enough to clear her."

"When we compare the recording of the simulation to the live footage, we can tell she fired many shots previous to that one," Keller said. "None of those were live fire, neither the hits nor the misses."

"And the other data doesn't show any sign of anything changing before that last shot," Wyss added. "No radio signals or anything that would've switched that gun from dormant to live. Admittedly, we haven't checked everything yet. Just the most obvious methods."

"Everyone else was on the ground," Keller said. "Except for you, of course."

"How long will it take you to search for all the less obvious methods?" Fitz asked.

"Days, maybe," Wyss said.

"There are some short-range things that might've triggered it, coming from Jeger's glider," Keller said.

"Are you seriously suggesting Jeger killed herself using Ritchie's gun?" Fitz asked.

"Well, or you," Keller said, unbothered by his growing annoyance.

"I didn't do it," Fitz said. But then added, "although check to be sure, okay? It would be nice to have more proof than my own word on that score."

"You think you're going to be a suspect, too?" Moreau asked.

"Some people already think I am," Fitz said darkly. "Also you, although I gather you're just considered an accomplice. Still, watch your back."

"Oh, that's nice," Moreau said.

Wyss went back over to the table and sat down beside Keller. They were both watching a constant scroll of text that was whipping by too fast for Fitz to follow, but they seemed to be having no trouble with it. He suspected they were scanning it, looking for some things in particular and ignoring the rest.

"Why are they detaining her, anyway?" Fitz grumbled to Moreau. "Do they think she's likely to do it again? Like she ever did in the first place."

"Like I said before. Officially, it's just because they haven't yet found any evidence to lend a reasonable doubt," Moreau said. "But unofficially? I think they—or at least Hansen—are worried what the other cadets will do. She does look guilty."

"So? Jeger wasn't exactly loved," Fitz said.

"She was still one of us, right?" Moreau said. "And one thing they drill into us is that we're closer than family. What harms one of us harms us all."

"And demands vengeance?" Fitz said.

"Some might think so. Especially if it looks like command is just going to let her get away with it," Moreau said.

"So we just need to give them something," Fitz said, tapping a fingertip on his lips as he thought. "We don't have to prove her innocent, not yet. They just need something to tell the cadets there's a possibility she didn't do it. Another suspect, maybe?"

"Are you thinking of something in specific?" Moreau asked.

"If we can prove the gun was tampered with, and that Ritchie couldn't possibly have done it, that might be a start," Fitz said, finger still tapping.

"I don't know, Fitz," Moreau said. "She was here all break with very little supervision. She could've done anything without being seen."

"Well, not anything," Wyss said, looking up from his scrolling text. "Our drones recorded all of her flights, for the data. Plus, the hangar has surveillance systems that run continuously."

"Can we compile everything to show she never touched the gun?" Fitz asked.

"All the way back through the break?" Moreau asked.

"Sure," Wyss said. "I can make a supercut of just her every time she's on the hangar deck, easy." He paused the scroll of text and wheeled his chair away from the holographic table to a computer station set in the corner of the room. The screen lit up at his approach, and his fingers reached for the input screen. They tapped away, entering a complex series of commands Fitz couldn't even understand, and he kept talking the whole time. "I don't have to stop at the beginning of break, either. I can take it all the way back to when she started last semester."

"Perfect," Fitz said. "That has to be proof, right?"

"I guess," Moreau said. "I just wish we had another suspect. A name we could give them."

"Once Ritchie is out of detention and part of our investigation, we'll find our suspect," Fitz said.

"You do realize there is an official investigation already underway?" Moreau asked with a hint of a smile. "This isn't a dead Felzkinder this time. It's a dead cadet, and a highly ranked one at that. People care."

"The official investigation isn't going to give all the cadets a blow by blow of how they're doing or what they're working on," Fitz said. "If we want them to stop suspecting Ritchie, or at least stop suspecting *just* Ritchie, that's on us."

"I have another idea," Keller said, pausing her own scroll of text then opening a new screen on the tabletop. "Maintenance records."

"I checked those already," Moreau said. "Remember? I did that first while you two were aggregating your data or whatever."

"I don't mean glider maintenance," Keller said with a dismissive wave of her hand. "I'm talking about that gun."

"We do maintenance on dummy guns?" Fitz asked.

"They're not dummies, remember? They're live laser cannons, just switched off," Keller said.

"But we never fire them. Up until today, I assumed they didn't even work," Fitz said.

"They work," Keller said. "There's a course in complex weapon maintenance, and the cadets in that class take the guns off the gliders and do a full disassembly, cleaning, and reassembly."

"Interesting," Fitz said. He came around the table to stand at Keller's shoulder, but as with Wyss, she was inputting strings of text that meant nothing to him and moving through screens of data faster than he could follow. "Can you tell when the last class was held?"

"I can tell you more than that," Keller said, and her fingers gave a few last, harder taps. "I can give you the name of the cadet who last touched the gun that's now on Ritchie's glider."

"Nicol Egli," Moreau read over her shoulder. Then she shook her head. "No, I don't think so."

"What do you mean?" Fitz asked. "Who's Nicol Egli?"

"Jeger's buddy," Moreau said. "But there's no way she's guilty. She was incredibly upset when she heard what had happened. There's no way she was acting."

"Anything's possible," Fitz said.

"Not this," Moreau said. "We have to find something else."

"No, this works," Fitz insisted. Moreau gave him a stony look, but he didn't relent. "Look, I'm not saying she's guilty. I'm just saying that with this piece of evidence, we can make her look just as likely to be guilty as Ritchie. And that's all we need, right?"

"Is it?" Moreau said, narrowing her eyes. "Too bad for Egli, I guess? And who's to say they even let Ritchie out? Maybe all we've done is give her a really miserable roommate in the detention cell."

"No, this will work," Fitz said. "Can you send that to my tablet?" Keller nodded and tapped at the screen.

"What are you going to do?" Moreau asked.

"I'm going to take this to Hansen," Fitz said. "He might not be in charge here, but I know he'll listen to me. I'm not sure that's true of any of the others. I met all of them over the course of last semester, and none of them like me much."

"You haven't exactly been making the most of your last chance at success, no," Moreau said.

"Hey," Fitz said, surprised to find himself feeling a little hurt by her words.

"Sorry."

"Maybe you're right," Fitz said. "But I can't fix that now. What I can do is talk to Hansen, and show him this, and maybe get Ritchie freed. And I'm not trying to do that at the expense of this cadet Egli. I don't see any reason why they both can't be free to attend classes until the official investigation is complete. I'm not going to slander this Egli. Is she a friend of yours?"

"Not particularly," Moreau said. "But I guess some of that 'we're closer than family' stuff is starting to rub off on me. I don't want to see another cadet be the victim of injustice. Not even if it saves my friend."

"Me neither," Fitz said. His tablet pinged to let him know Keller had sent him the file. "Okay. Wish me luck. Hopefully, when next I see you, Ritchie is with us."

11

RITCHIE WAS STILL POKING at the remains of her dinner when two guards came to her doorway. There had been a shift rotation since the last two had brought in her meal, apparently. These two were both young women, but no one she recognized. They were probably in their last year at the academy.

"Finished?" one of them asked.

"Pretty much," Ritchie said, pushing the plate away. She didn't have much of an appetite. But at least making an attempt at eating had been something to do. "Can I get the passcode for this desk? I'd like to catch up on the classes I missed today."

"No," the guard said. "You're actually being released. We're here to escort you back to the main hallway."

"Released? So they know who tampered with my glider?" Ritchie asked.

"No, not yet," the guard said. "But you're no longer the sole suspect."

"And I get released because of that?" Ritchie asked. "It sounds like someone else should be in here with me."

The guard shrugged. "I guess the thinking is we're about to have a lot of suspects, and we don't have room for you all."

"Plus, Colonel Hansen vouched for you," the other guard said, speaking up for the first time. "So don't do anything stupid."

"I won't. I just really want to get back to class," Ritchie said.

They walked Ritchie out of the cell and down the narrow hallway of the administrative wing, back to the larger central hall that led from the library, past the cafeteria and meeting rooms, to the entrance to the barracks.

"Thanks," Ritchie said, but neither of them answered.

Then she was alone. She could hear voices from the library behind her, but the cafeteria to her right was already dark and silent, even the after-dinner cleanup long since done.

She could go to the library, retrieve her assignments at any station at the study table, and get to work. But the idea of going into a room filled with her fellow cadets was too daunting. She could only imagine how hard the rumor mill had been churning while she was in detention. What were people saying of her?

She wondered who the other suspect was. But her social anxiety won out over her curiosity. She would be forced to deal with everyone tomorrow, anyway. No need to rush it. She turned the other way and headed down to her room in the barracks.

It was too early for anyone to be washing up before lights out, and most cadets were studying, but a few were chatting in the hallway. About what, Ritchie had no idea, but she was sure she could make a pretty good guess because every time she approached one of those groups, the talking ceased. Some of the cadets ignored her, but others gave her icy stares until she was passed. Then the whispers started up again.

Command might have considered her not suspicious enough to detain any longer, but clearly, the bulk of the cadets felt otherwise.

When she reached her room, she saw Frei working at her desk, Grof sprawled out on her bunk with her reader balanced on her chest, and Moreau pacing the floor with her head down.

"Er, hi," Ritchie said from the doorway. "I'm back."

Grof let her reader fall flat on her chest so she could look at Ritchie with raised eyebrows. "How was the detention cell?"

"I guess about what you would expect," Ritchie said. "Never thought I'd be in one myself."

Frei turned in her chair to give Ritchie a long look. Whatever she was thinking, it didn't show on her face. Just when Ritchie was about to break out in a nervous sweat, Frei finally relented and said, "welcome back." Then she turned back to her studying.

"Thanks," Ritchie said, then looked to Moreau. "I don't know what happened, but I'm guessing you and Fitz were involved?"

"And Keller and Wyss," Moreau said.

"The drone footage showed something?"

"No, but we were following a couple of different lines of inquiry," Moreau said. "Fitz got the idea to check on the maintenance records for the gun, not the glider. We don't have any evidence that anything in particular was done to it, but it did mean that we had the names of other people who need to be questioned."

"What names?" Ritchie asked.

"So far, just Egli," Moreau said. "And it doesn't mean she did anything, just that she had opportunity, maybe." Then her eyebrows drew down together in concern. "What did I say? You just went white."

Ritchie was about to answer when she heard the sound of Frei shifting her weight on her chair. It wasn't loud, but Ritchie knew what it was meant to convey. "Come on," she said softly. "Let's take this out into the hall."

Moreau followed her out of the room and a few meters away from the doorway.

"Don't want to be overheard?" Moreau asked when they came to a stop. "Must be juicy."

"No, I don't care who hears me, but Frei's trying to study."

"So tell me about Egli."

Ritchie gave Moreau a full accounting of what she had overheard that morning in the showers.

Had it really only been that morning? It felt like a lifetime ago.

"I don't know," Moreau said when she had finished. "That doesn't sound like much to go on."

"I don't think she did it," Ritchie said. "But she definitely knows something about Jeger that might be relevant. I'm going to go talk to her."

"We don't have a lot of time. It's almost lights out," Moreau said.

"'We?'"

"I'm coming with you, of course," Moreau said.

Ritchie didn't have to consult anything to know which room was Egli's. She had been Jeger's buddy, and Jeger had been the cadet captain for this wing of the barracks. That position came with responsibility, including keeping watch for anyone trying to sneak out of the barracks after hours, so her room was the one closest to the main hall.

That position also came with perks. The room was the same size as the one Ritchie and Moreau shared with Grof and Frei, but it was just Jeger and Egli sleeping there. They each had their own set of bunks and their own desk, and apparently a couple of spare lockers.

And now it was just Egli in there. Ritchie supposed someone would have to be appointed a new cadet captain. She wondered who it would be, and what would happen to the now buddy-less Egli.

"Knock knock?" Ritchie said from the doorway. Egli was sitting at one of the desks with her back to the door, but didn't turn around.

"I'm not a cadet captain," she said. She was no longer crying, but her voice had a thick, raw quality to it now. "Whatever you need, you're going to have to go down to the other barracks and find Bale."

"Actually, we wanted to talk to you," Ritchie said, and Egli's back stiffened. Apparently, this time she had realized who she was talking to. She turned in her chair to face the doorway.

"I don't want to talk," Egli said. "I have nothing more to say."

"But I have something I have to tell you," Ritchie said. Egli glowered for a minute, but then gave a little nod. Ritchie and Moreau came into the room. Moreau sat down on one of the neatly made bunks. Ritchie pulled the other desk chair over to sit as close to Egli as she dared. "Has anyone from command been in here to talk to you?"

"You mean like a therapist or something?" Egli asked, narrowing her eyes.

"No, not that," Ritchie said. "They let me out of detention because I'm no longer the only name on their list of suspects."

"Okay," Egli said slowly. Then, "wait, you mean they've added my name? What did you tell them?"

"Nothing! It wasn't me," Ritchie said, raising her hands in surrender. "Honestly. I didn't know anything about it until I got out."

"It was Cadet Fitz and me," Moreau said. "We found your name as the last one to perform strip down and maintenance on the laser cannon for Ritchie's glider."

"What?" Egli asked, pinching the bridge of her nose between her thumb and forefinger as if to stave off a building headache.

"It's flimsy; we know that," Moreau said. "And command knows that, which is why you've not been detained."

"Although I'm surprised no one's at least talked to you about it," Ritchie said.

"But I didn't do anything to that gun. I mean, only what I was supposed to. And that was half a semester ago!" Egli said.

"I know," Ritchie said. "I didn't do anything either. I know you don't believe me, but I swear it's true. And I honestly believe you're innocent, too. But someone in this academy isn't."

"Command will find them," Egli said.

"Sure, eventually," Ritchie said. "But by then, our reputations will be destroyed by the cadet rumor mill."

Egli scowled. "Like I even care about that now. My friend is dead."

"I'm sorry for that," Ritchie said. "Truly, I am." But Egli just narrowed her eyes again. Ritchie looked back at Moreau. "Why doesn't anyone believe me?"

But it was Egli who answered. "Because when Jeger breaks you down, you're supposed to cry in the showers. You're supposed to turn to your fellow cadets for support. You're not supposed to get that hard look on your face like the minute you have an opportunity, you're going to burn the whole school to the ground."

"So, everyone thinks I'm capable of murder because I don't cry?" Ritchie asked, annoyed.

"You could be a little human. Not so much super soldier in training," Egli said.

"Plus, you're wicked smart," Moreau added. "Everyone pretty much believes you could plot a murder and get away with it. Even one that involved you killing your victim in front of everyone and calling it an accident. It's actually kind of a compliment. People just think you're super competent."

"And completely lacking in any sort of moral compass," Ritchie said.

They all fell silent. Ritchie's thoughts were spiraling into a pit of frustrated depression, but Egli was just staring at her, chewing her lip as if mulling something over.

"Maybe I don't think you did it," Egli said. Then, when Ritchie straightened up in her chair, quickly added, "Maybe! But if it wasn't you, and I know it wasn't me, then who?"

"We're already looking into who had opportunity," Moreau said. "Keller and Wyss are going through all the academy's surveillance footage."

"Who are Keller and Wyss?" Egli asked with a frown.

"Novice cadets," Ritchie said. "They work together a lot on programs that are maybe a bit beyond their capabilities. But they're actually really smart. Just a shade too ambitious."

Egli was still frowning until Moreau added, "Keller is that girl who's always pestering Ritchie with questions about her dad and his work on translating really alien languages."

"Oh, her," Egli said. "And that pale kid who's always with her. Sure."

"Yeah, so if there's any record of anyone tampering with that gun, they'll find it. And that will clear you both," Moreau said.

"If they find anything at all," Ritchie said. "But there's one other way we can find who's behind this. We could figure out who had motive."

"Motive for murder?" Egli said. "It's just so extreme."

"People murder for all sorts of reasons," Moreau said with a shrug. "Passions run high."

"But this was extremely premeditated," Egli said.

"Agreed," Ritchie said. "Which was why I was hoping you could help with our investigation. You knew Jeger better than anyone. Was she having any sort of relationships with anyone that might have gone bad?"

Egli sat back in her chair, crossing her arms over her chest. "You're asking about what you heard this morning. I'm not talking about that."

"But it could be relevant," Ritchie said. "It might be relevant in a way that you don't see, but could become clear if we follow up on it."

"No," Egli said, even more firmly than before. "It was nothing. I promise you it was nothing."

"You both sounded pretty upset for it to have been nothing," Ritchie said as gently as she could.

"Well, it was," Egli said, getting up from her chair and walking towards the doorway. "It's nearly lights out. You two cadets should get back to your own room."

"If you could just tell us who you were talking about, we can leave you out of the rest of the investigation if you like," Ritchie said.

"I'm not telling you anything," Egli said, and her face was starting to flush with anger. "Look, my best friend is dead. If I thought what happened this morning was in any way relevant, I'd have already told command about it. But it wasn't. And I'm scarcely going to honor Jeger's memory by spilling all of her secrets now."

"We won't tell anyone," Ritchie said, but Egli just pointed towards the door. "Please?"

"We should go," Moreau said, getting up from the bunk and pulling Ritchie up out of the chair. "We're going to have to run to get into our room before lights out. The last thing we need is for you to be caught in Egli's room by a surveillance drone. That will look bad for both of you."

"Okay," Ritchie said, but paused in the doorway to speak to Egli one last time. "If you change your mind later, you know where to find me."

Egli scowled, but nodded. Ritchie hoped she would change her mind, but she didn't want to count on it.

And as she lay awake in her bunk staring up at the stone ceiling above her, she had to admit that without knowing who Egli and Jeger had been arguing about, she had no other leads. She could only hope Keller and Wyss found something useful.

12

THIS TIME when Fitz got to the cafeteria door, again before they were even open for breakfast service, he only had to wait a moment before Moreau and Ritchie joined him. Ritchie looked wrecked, her eyes red-rimmed and her complexion wan.

It was just the three of them. It hadn't been just the three of them since they arrived at school and stood on the train platform together, waiting for, as it turned out, Jeger and Bale.

Everything he had wanted to tell her was bursting to come out, but it wasn't the right time. Not even to get Ritchie's take on Jeger's war fears.

He desperately wanted Ritchie's take on Jeger's war fears.

But it wasn't the time. First, they had to clear Ritchie's name. Then Ritchie needed to get a decent night's sleep. Then, maybe, they'd find another perfect moment like this one again.

Moreau pointed to the back of the cafeteria, and Fitz nodded. The three of them crossed the darkened room.

"Everything okay?" Fitz asked her when they finally sat down around a table in the back corner of the room.

"Yeah," Ritchie said absentmindedly. But he didn't believe she had even really heard his question.

"Did they interrogate you yesterday?" he asked.

That seemed to snap her awake. "No. I mean, they asked questions, but I wasn't tortured or anything." She shot Moreau a questioning look.

"You do look a little pale," Moreau said.

"Oh," Ritchie said, touching her fingertips to her face as if she could feel the lack of color. "I didn't sleep well."

"We'll figure this out," Fitz promised her. "Now that we can work together, no problem, right?"

"I mean, command is investigating," Ritchie said.

"Yeah, but we don't want to wait for them, do we?" he asked. Ritchie just shrugged. Then the foodservice windows opened with loud clangs all at once.

"No, she doesn't," Moreau said for her. Then she got up from her chair. "I'll grab something for all of us. Ritchie, fill Fitz in about Egli."

"Who's Egli?" Fitz asked.

"Jeger's buddy," Ritchie said. "I overheard the two of them arguing about something yesterday morning in the showers. I don't know what exactly, but it involved a 'him.' I asked Egli about it last night, but she says it was nothing. Not relevant." She said the last two words distinctly, and he guessed they were a direct quote.

"Then that's two arguments Jeger had yesterday before class," Fitz said. "When everyone else was still at breakfast, I was on the hangar deck looking over my glider. Bale and Jeger came out of the command center arguing about her... motivational techniques."

"Bale would never do this," Ritchie said.

"Barring some huge—and hugely unexpected—personal revelation about him, I'd have to agree," Fitz said.

"You think he's the 'him?'"

"I guess it depends on what they meant by 'him.'"

"'You tell him or I will,'" Ritchie quoted.

"Tell him what?" Fitz asked.

"No clue," Ritchie sighed, propping her chin on one of her hands and letting her eyes slide half-closed. She looked exhausted.

Moreau came back to the table with an icy stare on her face, which Fitz momentarily thought was directed at him, like he was supposed to be making Ritchie feel better or something. Then he looked back over his shoulder and saw a group of cadets lingering in the cafeteria doorway, whispering together and shooting furtive looks at Ritchie. When they saw Moreau glaring at them, they fell silent, then got into the line for food.

"Here," Moreau said, setting down the tray and distributing mugs of steaming coffee and plates heaping with eggs and bacon in front of each of them.

"Thanks," Ritchie said, perking up again.

"So, what about the tone?" Fitz asked after chewing and swallowing an enormous forkful of egg. "When... was it Egli who said, 'if you don't tell him I will?'" Ritchie nodded. "So, did it sound like a professional clash or a personal one?"

"I guess personal, but who knows?" Ritchie said. "Until she's ready to tell us more, I don't know what to do with that information. Do you think Bale knows anything?"

"About Egli?"

"Well, I was thinking about Jeger."

Now it was Fitz's turn to shrug. "If I see him, I'll try to get a word with him. But it's not like Egli and Jeger had that argument, and then Jeger went out to find Bale. They're both cadet captains. It's part of their job to meet up before flight classes to go over the planned instruction, and I suppose divvy up the teams."

"He and Jeger spent a lot of time together, though," Ritchie said. "He must know her nearly as well as Egli. If Egli won't talk to us, maybe he will."

"I'll try to find him," Fitz said.

"I'll see if I can find Keller and Wyss," Moreau said. "See if they have any updates."

"Good," Ritchie said.

"What are you going to do?" Fitz asked.

"Go to class," Ritchie said, pushing back her empty plate and draining the last of her coffee. Then she said, "I can't miss any more classes. It's day two, and I'm already starting my fresh semester behind. I can't have a repeat of last semester."

"You won't," Fitz said. He wanted to add that there was no way this semester would be as hard for her as the last now that Jeger wasn't going to be there, making her miserable at every opportunity, but he bit the words back. Even he knew that was insensitive.

"See you at dinner?" she said, pointing first at Fitz and then at Moreau. Moreau raised a hand and nodded, her mouth full.

"If not before," Fitz said. He turned to watch as Ritchie made her way out of the cafeteria, winding a path through tables full of cadets leaning in close together and whispering and not being subtle about looking her way. She ignored them all. "It's like she doesn't even notice," he said to himself.

"She does," Moreau said between forkfuls of egg. "She works hard to look like she doesn't."

"I swear, if anyone says anything to her, I'm going to end up in detention myself," Fitz said, punching a fist into his open palm.

"I'll join you," Moreau said. "Actually, I'll probably be there first."

"Maybe, but mine will be the bigger infraction," Fitz said.

She got up from the table but put her hand on his shoulder before walking away. "I'll concede. You have a lot more practice at breaking the rules than I do. I bow to the master."

Fitz shared most of his classes with Moreau and Ritchie, but given they had been assigned seats when they had started at the academy based on barrack assignments, they were nowhere near each other. And given that he had no buddy, Fitz sat alone at a table designed for two. That felt lonelier today than it had before.

Bale, being two years ahead of them, wasn't in any of their classes unless he was leading a combat exercise. Fitz had hoped to see him at hand-to-hand drills, but he wasn't there. The rumor mill was whispering that he had been pulled from classes to assist with the investigation. So it didn't seem likely that Fitz was going to run into him at all.

After hand-to-hand drills, he and the other cadets all went back to the barracks to shower. Then Fitz went to his room to dress and make a stab at studying before dinner. When he got to the room, he found Stucki hunched over his desk, mumbling to himself as his fingers drummed on the surface of the desk. Imhof was nowhere in sight.

"Where's Imhof?" Fitz asked as he opened his locker.

"Dressed already. He hit the library," Stucki said with the distracted quality of someone saying one set of words while thinking of something else. Fitz could see that he wanted to study. Stucki didn't have the greatest memory in the world, but so far as Fitz had seen, he worked twice as hard to make up for it. It would be a kindness to let him be.

But Fitz just couldn't do it. "Say, do you know that cadet Egli?" he asked as he thrust his arms into a shirt.

"Egli?" Stucki said with a frown. "Is she in our class?"

"She's a last-year," Fitz said. "Jeger's buddy."

"Oh, her," Stucki said. "I would say I know her to nod to, but then as we've just discovered, I don't even know her name, so..." he trailed off with a vague hand gesture.

"Well, you're terrible at names," Fitz said good-naturedly.

"True," Stucki admitted.

"I'm just curious if she's come up in the whisper network at all," Fitz said as casually as he could. "I don't really have access to that, you know."

"These days, that's probably for the best. It's all mean-spirited nonsense," Stucki said. "But no, I haven't heard any talk about her. Why?"

"Just curious," Fitz said, dragging his hands through his still-wet hair until it was laying right.

"Curious about what?" Stucki asked suspiciously.

"Well, she was Jeger's buddy," Fitz said. "And she's been acting kind of shifty."

"Shifty? No," Stucki said. "She's grieving. That's what you're seeing."

"Is it?" Fitz said skeptically. "I guess, maybe. That's fair. But still. She might know something about Jeger that the rest of us don't."

"I expect she does," Stucki said.

"Secrets that she's not sharing, for instance."

"Well," Stucki said, slow and drawn out. "That's just what buddies do. They keep each other's confidences. I've told Imhof things I haven't even told my own brothers back home."

"Really?" Fitz asked. "Imhof?"

"I know you two haven't hit it off," Stucki said. "But he's a good guy, really. And hey, I'm sorry for bringing up the buddy thing. I know you don't have one. I imagine that's a drag."

"I've had buddies before," Fitz said as airily as he could. "I know what the relationship is like."

"Well... no offense?" Stucki said preemptively.

"Go on," Fitz prompted.

"Look, this isn't your first academy. You've been to—what?—all the others? That's a lot of buddies, and not a lot of time for bonding."

"Fair enough," Fitz said. "What's your point?"

"Egli and Jeger have been matched up for nearly four years now."

"Wait a minute," Fitz said. "Jeger wasn't always stationed here. She went to one of my former academies. She was there at the same time as me. Which one was it? I don't remember now."

"I don't know, but Egli was there too," Stucki told him. "Jeger was transferred about this time last year because command—and here I mean the real upper-level administrators—thought she had leadership potential. But the academy she was at already had a lot of good candidates for cadet captain. So she came here and really had no competition in getting that position."

"Egli transferred *here*? Just to stay buddies with Jeger?" Fitz asked. It was almost more than he could believe. "This place is a hellhole. And she did it to help Jeger advance?"

"I told you, man. They're tight," Stucki said.

Then he turned back to his desk and got back into the flow of whatever he was trying to memorize. Fitz didn't remember getting any homework that morning that even required remembering anything, but it was possible that was just because he hadn't been paying enough attention.

Fitz sat down at his own unshared desk and called up his home screen. But then he just sat there staring at it, unable to choose which task to complete first. Homework was the last thing his mind wanted to focus on.

But until dinnertime, there was nothing else he could do. Hopefully, Ritchie and Moreau found some sort of lead in the meantime.

13

RITCHIE HAD ALWAYS CONSIDERED herself a very disciplined sort of person. She never slept past an alarm, was never late for anything, and always turned her full attention to whatever task was at hand.

But after staring at the same screen of text on the library desktop for the better part of an hour, she just couldn't make herself study.

Not that there was anything else she *could* do. She and Fitz and Moreau had gone over everything they knew at dinner, but all they knew were dead ends. Until Egli talked or Keller and Wyss found something useful, all the three of them could do was wait.

But waiting wasn't an activity that should take all of your time. You did other things to distract yourself from the waiting. Things like homework. Because waiting all on its own was just sitting and breathing.

Ritchie had told herself this a dozen times. Every part of her mind was in total agreement. But every time she looked down at the screen, nothing happened. It was like she could no longer take in any sort of information.

The helpless waiting feeling was quickly getting crowded out by the more desperate feeling of falling behind on the second day of the semester. She had to get it together.

"Ritchie?"

Ritchie looked up, pushing the too-long hair from her eyes, and saw Keller standing hesitantly beside her chair.

"News?" Ritchie asked, straightening up.

"News?" Keller repeated as if she wasn't sure what the word referred to.

"With that thing you and Wyss were doing. To find out who sabotaged my glider and laser cannon," she said, trying not to let all of her irritated impatience show in her voice.

"Oh, that," Keller said with a laugh. "No. I mean, I don't think so. That's more Wyss's thing."

"Then what did you want to tell me?" Ritchie asked. Was it Fitz? Or Moreau? Did they need her? Was this strange little girl completely failing at the task of summoning her quickly?

"Well, it's not so much tell you as ask you," Keller said, twisting her hands together.

"You need to know more about what happened up there?" Ritchie asked. "I've repeated that story so many times, but I don't think I've left anything out."

"No, it's not that," Keller said. "I wanted to ask you about the gaseous species of the Vien District."

Ritchie stopped holding back her emotions. She let every bit of irritation furrow her brow and shoot out of her eyes.

But it did no good. Keller just kept talking. "I know you said you don't remember, but if you could just try. Any little thing might be just the breakthrough we need."

"I have nothing for you," Ritchie said darkly.

"Are you sure? Well, that's a shame," Keller said with a little pout. "I wish you could've gone home over the break and found your father's notes like we discussed. I mean, I understand you wanted to work harder at combat flight. I'm not judging! Just wishing."

"We didn't discuss that," Ritchie said. "You kept trying to discuss it, and I kept saying no. I don't even know where my mother put my father's things. And I'm not going to ask." She said that last bit even more forcefully, but Keller was undeterred.

"Yeah, I remember," she said. "Well, I had another thing to ask you about, and this one I know didn't happen when you were a kid. It's about that last mission your father went on to try to negotiate with the Yuffids."

"No," Ritchie said, but her anger was starting to deflate. Keller had never brought this up specifically before, but Ritchie had always feared the day she would. But why did that day have to be today of all days?

"Their form of communication is very intriguing," Keller said. "No one knows how much of it is verbal and how much of it is gestures and body language. That's probably why it all went so wrong in the end. He had that balance wrong. Too much gesture, not enough speech. Or maybe the other way around."

"I'm not having this conversation," Ritchie said, shutting off the library screen and getting up from her chair.

"Wait!" Keller cried and grabbed hold of her wrist to hold her there.

Ritchie just stared at those pudgy hands wrapped around her wrist. They looked so small. Chubby. Kids' hands, really. And yet, in that moment, Ritchie couldn't escape. How could Keller not feel her trembling? It was all Ritchie could do to hold herself together.

"Can you tell me about how he prepared for that meeting?" she asked. There was a hungry gleam in her eyes, like a predator that has nearly taken down its prey. "I've read everything about it I could find, but you were actually there."

"Let go of me, Keller," Ritchie said. She had hoped those words would come out more commanding than they did.

"Come on! I know you don't like to talk about it, but this is part of my education. I can learn so much from what you know," Keller said, still gripping Ritchie's hand.

"Keller!" Wyss cried out as he ran into the library. He sounded appalled, but the look Keller gave him was pure confusion with a little bit of hurt because he had yelled at her.

"What?" she asked. "What did I do?"

"You're doing it now," Wyss said, reaching out to pry Keller's hands off Ritchie's wrist. "We talked about this. You have to let it go. Ritchie doesn't want to talk about this stuff. Ever! Look at her, Keller."

Keller looked up at Ritchie and seemed to finally see her for the first time. Ritchie wiped at her face and felt the dampness of tears.

"I'm sorry," Keller said in a small, contrite voice. "I got carried away."

"You always do," Wyss sighed.

"I'm sorry," Keller said again to Ritchie. Then she ran from the library.

"She's obsessed," Wyss said, running his hands over his whitish-blond hair. "And sometimes I think not in a good way."

"Thanks," Ritchie said. "Did you need something?"

"Me? No, I was just passing by. I just left our meeting room. I've been given strict orders not to doze off in there," he said. "I fell asleep a few times last semester and missed curfew."

"What are you working on in there now?"

"I'm still tweaking the program I've created to search all the surveillance videos," Wyss said. "I'm compiling a list of everyone who was anywhere near either your glider or the laser cannon that's mounted to your glider since last year."

"And?" Ritchie asked.

"It's a long list," he admitted. "I'm working my way back to the day that Jeger started here as a student, and then I'm going to examine every incident one by one. Time-consuming as hell, but I think in the end, I'll have something."

"I hope so," Ritchie said. "Can I see what you have so far? Maybe something will trigger something in me when I see it."

"I'd love to, but I really can't now," Wyss said, and he was already walking backwards towards the door to the main hall. "Like I said, strict orders."

"Not to sleep in the library meeting room," Ritchie said, getting up to follow him before he was out of reach of her voice.

"Not me specifically this time, though," Wyss said and waited for her to reach him before walking together with her down the long hall to the smaller barracks corridors.

"What do you mean?" Ritchie asked.

"There is now a zero-tolerance policy against being out of bed after lights out," Wyss said. "I bet when you get downstairs, you'll find that's true on your side as well."

"Because of Jeger?" Ritchie asked. But what would a strict curfew at bedtime have to do with that mid-morning accident?

"No," Wyss said. "Actually, there's a cadet who's gone missing."

"Who?" Ritchie asked.

"A last-year kid by the name of Kung," Wyss said. "I don't know him."

"Me neither," Ritchie said.

"I guess he's been missing since yesterday, but nobody noticed until after dinner today?" Wyss said. "How that could happen, I don't know. I've skipped my fair share of classes, and I can promise you, they always notice."

"Was someone covering for him somehow?" Ritchie asked.

"Interesting. Maybe," Wyss said.

"Do you know what time yesterday he went missing?" Ritchie asked. They had reached the place where the corridors to the two halves of the barracks diverged. He stopped at the top of his sloping hallway to answer her.

"I knew you'd ask me that," he said and seemed to be fighting the urge to smile. "I've heard different accounts, either of which might be wrong. But what folks are saying is that he disappeared either right before or right after the accident."

"Are you sure?" Ritchie asked, grabbing his arm. A bit too tightly, to judge by the flinch he didn't quite manage to hide.

"No, of course I'm not sure," Wyss said indignantly. "This is the realm of rumor, not the realm of science. But I bet you could do some digging and find some better answers. Not now, of course. We're running out of time before lights out."

He was looking pointedly down at her hand, and she released his arm with a murmured apology.

As she watched him run down the other barracks corridor until he disappeared from sight, she was completely tempted to try following him. She wasn't supposed to be on that side of things, and rumor said there were measures in place to keep any cadet from trying it. Security systems. Painful ones. The details varied.

But she really wanted to talk to Fitz about this guy Kung. She had no classes with last-year cadets, save the combat flight exercises which were led by the two cadet captains. She had no idea who Kung was or what he looked like. Did Fitz know him at all?

Then the lights started to flicker, her last warning before every hallway was going to be armed with painful security measures to punish cadets still out of bed.

She turned and sprinted down the other hall to her own room.

14

AT FIRST, finding Ritchie already up and waiting for him at the cafeteria door was a pleasant surprise for Fitz. Then he got closer and saw just how worn out she looked. He guessed she'd just passed a second sleepless night.

Not that he had slept so well himself. Still, he was certain he didn't look as bad as she did.

"Hey," he said. "Where's Moreau?"

"In the shower still," Ritchie said. "She'll be up in a minute."

"Do you want to grab a table?" he asked, gesturing to the empty cafeteria. She nodded, and he led the way to the same table they had taken the day before. "I wished command would say something," he said when it became clear that Ritchie wasn't going to speak first. "They are running an investigation that has access to tools we don't. Scientific tools. Professional ones. So what's taking them so long to figure out who did this?"

Ritchie just shrugged and pushed the hair back from her face. Fitz felt a little stab in his heart. She was no longer striving to stay within regulations. That wasn't like her.

And weirdly, seeing her opening flaunting regs made him actually miss Jeger. Which shouldn't be possible.

"Do you know anything about a last-year cadet named Kung?" she asked.

"Kung? I don't think so," Fitz said. "Do you think he's going to get promoted to the open cadet captain slot?"

"No, I don't think so. Wyss said he's been missing since yesterday. Wait, the day before yesterday," she amended.

"Missing? You think someone would've said something about that," Fitz said.

"Apparently, there is now a zero-tolerance policy for being up and about after lights out," Ritchie said. "Like, not even the library. I know why I don't know anything about it. My side of the barracks is short a cadet captain to tell us these things. I'm surprised no one has stepped up. But how did Wyss, a novice cadet, know about this, and you didn't?"

Fitz rubbed at the back of his neck and gave Ritchie an uncomfortable grin. Did he have to tell out to her how out of the loop he was? "I must've missed it when the word passed around. I haven't seen Bale around much," he said. "I still wanted to talk to him about Jeger, you know?"

"Well, I think we should try to find where this Kung guy could've gone," Ritchie said. "Maybe he should be on the list of suspects."

"Where would we even start?" Fitz asked. "Command would've done everything obvious already. If he was anywhere surveillance cameras or drones could find him, they'd have him."

"Yes, and I suppose we have to assume they're actively looking for him, because why wouldn't they?" Ritchie said with a sigh. "Maybe we can figure out who his friends are. Ask them some questions."

"Friends, or better yet, his buddy," Fitz said. He accessed the room assignments on his implant. "Vilem Blaser. I don't know him either." He sent Blaser's official photo over to Ritchie's implant and watched as her eyes went out of focus, then focused back on him again. "Distinctive, right? Dark skin and platinum hair. No way we're going to miss seeing him, even in a crowd."

"Let's go by the door," Ritchie said. "We can catch him when he comes in."

Cadets were starting to come up the hallway towards the cafeteria, but none of them were Blaser.

One of them, however, was Moreau.

"Who are we looking for?" she asked as she took a position next to Ritchie and also scanned the oncoming crowd.

"Cadet Blaser," Fitz said, sending the photo to Moreau's implant.

"Kung's buddy," Ritchie said. Moreau made an affirmative noise; clearly, Ritchie had already filled her in on all of it the night before. He felt more left out than ever, not having a bunkmate to talk to after lights out.

They waited and watched. At one point, Moreau ducked inside and got egg sandwiches for all of them so they could eat while standing. Technically against regulations to eat outside the cafeteria, but Fitz didn't care. And as he watched Ritchie toss her hair out of her face again, he didn't think she did either.

Then everyone started leaving again, heading to the first class of the morning.

"Is he still in bed?" Ritchie asked. "Or in detention? Or hiding with his buddy or what?" She sounded frustrated, and the lack of sleep wasn't helping her keep the grumpiness out of her voice.

"We'll find him," Fitz said. "His first class is advanced navigation. That's in room... 41B. I know where that is." He started off, Ritchie falling into step beside him. But then she stopped to look at Moreau, who was on her other side.

"I don't think we should all go," she said to her. "There's no way we're making it to class on time."

"So I'm supposed to sit through the 'Cadet Moreau, where is your buddy?' lecture all on my own?" Moreau asked.

"Sorry?" Ritchie said.

"I would think you'd want to be there, after missing so many classes the first day," Moreau grumbled.

"Take good notes for me," Ritchie said.

"Wait, are you planning on being late or being absent?" Moreau asked.

"We'll have to play it by ear," Fitz said, tugging at Ritchie's sleeve. "Let's go."

They left Moreau behind, racing through the emptying hallways to get to the navigation classroom. It was laid out like the bridge of a ship, only in this case, every station served the same function. The teacher was standing in the middle of the room near what looked like a ship captain's chair, barking instructions as cadets raced to get their stations online. Luckily, his back was to the door.

"Do you see him?" Fitz asked, scanning every cadet. Some of them he saw in profile, but most were also sitting with their backs to him.

"No," Ritchie said, stepping back from the door before they got caught and bawled out. "Definitely no sign of that hair. Assuming that's a current picture?"

"Assuming," Fitz agreed. "So, he's cutting class as well."

"Maybe he's in the infirmary," Ritchie said. "Or detention. Command could be questioning him about Kung themselves, you know."

Fitz nodded, but he wasn't ready to give up the hunt. Mostly because as late as they were for class, it was better at this point to miss it all together. But he wasn't entirely sure that even this new devil-may-care Ritchie would see it that way.

"Let's check his bunk," Fitz said.

"I can't go down there," Ritchie said, even as she followed him back down the hall.

"What are you talking about? Of course, you can," he said.

"No, there are systems in place," Ritchie said. "Cadets assigned to one wing of the barracks can't enter the other wing. Everyone knows that."

"Everyone knows," Fitz scoffed. "It's easy to keep everyone in line with what everyone knows."

"Huh?"

"Just trust me," he said. But she didn't follow him down the corridor. He had to go back and hold out his hand to her. "I promise you. I've done this a million times."

"I've never seen you in our wing of the barracks," she said, narrowing her eyes skeptically.

"Well, I've not done it *here*," he said. "I'm trying to behave on

Oymyakon, remember? Present circumstances excepted. But all academies work the same. Trust me. You'll be fine."

Ritchie stared at his outstretched hand for an eternity. In the end, she didn't take it, but she did start walking down the corridor. He fell in step beside her.

"You better not be wrong," she said.

But a quick search of the barracks turned up nothing more than cleaning robots still scrubbing the showers. No one was downstairs. And every bunk had been neatly made.

"Where else?" Fitz asked, tapping his lips with his finger as they walked back up to the main hall.

"Library, I guess," Ritchie said. "Maybe we need to find a closer link between this guy and us. Someone we know who might know one of his friends or something. This feels so random."

"I would love to do that," Fitz said. "Sadly, I have no such friends."

"Maybe I could try Egli again," Ritchie suggested.

They reached the library and looked over every cadet who had a free hour to spend studying. None of them had platinum blond hair or dark skin.

"Egli is probably in class," Fitz said as they walked back out again.

"Maybe we should be too," Ritchie sighed.

They were just passing the cafeteria again when Fitz saw a shadow move. No, not a shadow. It was a silhouette behind the opaqued glass of one of the meeting rooms. He glanced over at Ritchie, who had clearly seen it too. They crept up to the door, and Fitz gently eased it open.

At first, all he could see were mountains of equipment piled up on the conference table that dominated the room. Then he heard something move, like one of those mountains shifting, little bits grinding against other little bits in a metallic clamor.

Then someone on the other side of the central mountain sat back. Someone with platinum blonde hair.

"Cadet Blaser?" he said as he stepped into the room. Ritchie followed him, softly closing the door behind them.

"Who wants to know?" Blaser asked, not looking up from whatever he was doing.

"Cadets Fitz and Ritchie," Fitz said.

"I don't know any... wait, did you say Ritchie?"

"Yeah," Fitz said, shooting Ritchie a sympathetic look. Lots of people recognized her name, and while few were as annoying about it as he knew Cadet Keller to be, he had seen how much it pained her when people said her name but thought of her father.

"The one who killed Jeger?" Blaser asked.

Fitz glanced over at Ritchie. This new notoriety attached to her name was no improvement for her; he could tell by the way she flinched.

"It wasn't her," Fitz said. "She was just the instrument."

"I was used," Ritchie said, and her voice was thick with emotion. They had come far enough around the table to see Blaser full-on now. He sat back in his chair with his arms folded, looking Ritchie over carefully. Then he seemed to come to a decision, turning his attention back to whatever it was he was working on.

"Yeah, I guess I can see how that could be true," he said. He turned a part over in his hands, examining it. Fitz had no idea what it was a part to. "Command certainly doesn't think she did it, so I guess that's something."

"They don't?" Ritchie asked breathlessly.

Blaser looked up at her again. "Well, I assumed you knew that since they let you go and everything."

"No. No one said a word about ruling me out," Ritchie said.

Blaser just shrugged and dropped a pair of magnifying spectacles in front of his eyes to even more closely examine the part in his hands.

"What are you doing?" Fitz asked. "I mean, you're supposed to be in class."

"Punishment," Blaser said. "I will be in this room until every single one of these boards passes quality checks. They're currently all broken in a fun variety of ways."

Fitz gave a low whistle. "That's a lot of boards."

"Yeah, well." Blaser shrugged again. He was about to turn his attention back to his work when he looked up at the two of them. "You know, maybe you shouldn't be in here. You might get me in even more trouble if you're caught. And just why are you here, anyway? Don't you have class?"

Fitz ignored that last question. "Actually, we're looking for Cadet Kung," he said. "Have you seen him?"

Blaser looked up, not at them, but closer to the ceiling. As if glancing at surveillance cameras, although none were visible. Clearly, he thought he was being watched.

Well, they almost certainly *were* being watched.

"They've already asked you about this, haven't they?" Fitz guessed.

Blaser gave the smallest of nods. "That's how I know they don't think Ritchie did it. Because now they think Kung did. But he wouldn't. Especially not Jeger."

"Why especially not her?" Ritchie asked. Fitz saw the gleam in her eye. She thought she had found the elusive 'him.'

But Blaser didn't answer. The board in front of him had all of his attention again.

"Look, Blaser," Fitz said, pulling out a chair so he could sit down and look Blaser in the eye. "We don't think Kung did it either. We just want to help. Can you tell us why he's hiding? Is he in danger, too?"

"He's been down there since before Jeger was even killed," Blaser said, then flushed as he realized just what he had said.

"Down where?" Ritchie asked, and Fitz could tell she was trying not to sound too eager.

"I said too much," Blaser said, biting down on his lip.

"You know where he is, then," Fitz said. "You've seen him since Jeger died?"

"No, I haven't," Blaser said, glancing up at the ceiling again. "At first he said he just needed some time, and so I let him go alone. Then all this happened, but I didn't hear about it until after dinner, and by that time command knew that Kung was missing. Then I couldn't go, not without leading them straight to him."

"If he's innocent, he should come out," Ritchie said gently. "Hiding makes him look guilty. Unless, like Fitz said, he's in danger?"

"No, he's not in any danger," Blaser said. "I think you're right. He probably needs to come back up now. I was hoping he'd come up on his own, though. If they see me go and get him, they'll know I lied when I said I didn't know where he was."

"You could tell us where he is, and we could go get him for you," Fitz suggested.

"No," Blaser said, taking off the magnifying spectacles and setting them on the table. "It's better if I'm the one who tells him about Jeger."

Ritchie leaned forward, and Fitz sensed she was going to ask just what was going on between Kung and Jeger. He turned and looked up at her and gave her a small shake of his head.

She frowned, but then she nodded.

"Lead away," Fitz said to Blaser.

15

BLASER LED them down the main hallway away from the library towards the part of the school that was deeper under the mountain.

Deeper under the mountain. Not somewhere she wanted to go. But the lights were bright, and the walls were paneled and the floors tiled. If she tried really hard, she could pretend she was still in a normal building, up on the surface of the planet and not under untold tons of stone.

They were just passing the corridors to the barracks when Moreau stepped out of the shadows to fall into step beside them.

"I thought you were staying in class," Ritchie said.

"I did. Class is done," Moreau said. "I have some time before lunch. And I took extra good notes to try to replicate your usual exhaustive methods."

"Oh. Thanks," Ritchie said, a bit embarrassed for how aggressive she had sounded earlier.

"So, what are we doing?" Moreau asked as they continued walking past classroom after classroom.

"Following Blaser," Ritchie said.

"I got that much," Moreau said and rolled her eyes. "But where?"

"To where Kung is hiding," Ritchie said. "Somewhere under the school, apparently. Do you know of anything under the school?"

"I would've thought there was nothing beneath us but a mountain of stone," Moreau said. "Is there a basement or something? I've never seen it. I've never even seen a door that looked like it could go to a basement."

"Me neither," Ritchie said. "I don't know how long this is going to take, though. Maybe you should stay up here, so someone knows where we've gone."

"Oh, no. You're not getting rid of me twice," Moreau said. "If we're not back by the end of lunch, we'd just be missing hand to hand combat drills. My notes on that aren't going to be any help to you. We will most definitely be missed, though."

"Can't be helped, I guess," Ritchie said, rubbing tiredly at her eyes. "I really hope we learn something helpful from Kung. I have *got* to get a better night of sleep tonight."

The larger hallway came to a dead end, but there was a smaller hall that jutted off perpendicularly to the left, and Blaser led the way down this. They were no longer walking past classroom doors. These doors were smaller and bore the softly flashing red lights of locking mechanisms.

"Where are we?" Ritchie whispered to Fitz, who was walking a bit ahead of her. But it was Blaser who answered her.

"These are storerooms," he said. "I don't know what's in them. I've never run across anyone from the faculty going in or out of them, but then again, it's usually the middle of the night when I come down this way."

"The middle of the night?" Ritchie said. "Aren't you afraid of getting caught?"

Fitz looked back at her and shook his head bemusedly.

"It's not a stupid question," Ritchie said, mostly to herself.

The hall took another ninety-degree turn and started running downhill at an almost uncomfortably steep angle. The lights were dimmer and more widely spaced as well, and Ritchie could feel a cold dampness eking out of the stone around her, sinking into her bones. It was hard to tune out the thought of all the stone above her, waiting to crush her like a bug.

They passed one last set of doors, and then the hallway just ended.

But Blaser dropped to one knee and started fumbling with something Ritchie couldn't see. They had left the last of the lights behind at the last set of doors. It was getting harder to pretend she was in a building on the surface, perfectly safe and not about to be crushed by falling rock.

There was a metallic clang, and Blaser disappeared from her view. Then Fitz got to his knees. It was only when he crawled forward, also disappearing into the darkness, that Ritchie realized there was a grate, unfastened on the bottom. It shut with another clang, and Ritchie got to her knees to hoist it back up again.

She hoped they didn't have to crawl far. It was hard enough tuning out her claustrophobia in the big spaces without having to get into a crawlspace.

To her relief, they only had to crawl for about a meter, and then they were standing again in another identical hallway with widely dispersed, dim lights.

"Is that water?" Moreau asked as she emerged behind Ritchie, pointing at where the floor met the wall. It did look particularly slick there, a sheen that barely reflected the dim lights.

"Yeah," Blaser said. "I think there's a reason this part of the fortress was abandoned."

"Wait, fortress?" Ritchie asked.

"Yeah, this place used to be a fortress," Blaser said. "Like eons ago."

"More like centuries," Fitz said. "And I don't think it ever saw much action."

The sheen of water was now a trickle that ran down the center of the hall. And it wasn't a recent development. It had been running long enough to wear a groove into the center of the floor, a little channel in the stone.

"We're almost there," Blaser said as the hall took yet another turn and continued down into actual darkness this time.

"Wait," Ritchie said as she stopped. She made the mistake of touching one of the walls and had to run her wet, gritty palm down the side of her pants to get it clean again. "It's dark down there."

"Just turn your night vision on with your implant," Moreau said.

"That's just outlines and stuff," Ritchie said. "There could be all sorts of things down there we don't see. Small creepy crawly things. Squishy things."

"I have a light," Fitz said, digging in his pocket and producing a small glow stick. He clicked it on, and it filled the hallway with a soft green light. It was designed to work with the night vision her implant superimposed on her normal vision, providing extra information without blinding her.

"Thanks," Ritchie said.

"I never would've pegged you as afraid of the dark," Moreau said. Ritchie appreciated the fact that she whispered this very close to her ear and didn't just announce it to the whole group.

"Dark on a spaceship or a station is fine," Ritchie said. "This is different."

"Cave dark," Moreau said with a nod. "Yeah, not my favorite either. Thanks for asking for the light. I don't think I would've spoken up."

"Oh. Well, you're welcome," Ritchie said.

The hall was no longer taking perpendicular turns. They were hairpins now, zigzagging back and forth like a ramp meant to replace a staircase. Ritchie tried really hard not to imagine just how deep they were going.

Then she saw a light up ahead, not a green glow stick one and not the dim lights like in the hallway above. This was a warm, yellow glow flooding the hallway from some place off to the right. Blaser turned into it, followed by Fitz. Then Ritchie and Moreau were stepping into the same space.

It was a large room, its stone walls squared off but left bare, without panels or tiles. The air was cold and damp, but at least there was no standing water on the floor. The light was coming from a lantern set on top of an overturned plastic crate. It was the sort of lantern the cadets used when they camped outside while on tactical hikes. It could be shuttered and turned down to a deep red glow to provide just enough illumination for those on watch. Currently, it was fully open and cranked to the highest illumination setting.

It still didn't reach into the shadows that hid the ceiling above them.

Ritchie gazed up into that darkness for several minutes before dropping her eyes to the floor, which was strewn with squares of paper. Some appeared blank, but others were covered with markings. She bent to pick one up and saw a roughly drawn portrait of Cadet Captain Jeger. She picked up another and saw yet another portrait, this one from a different angle. She realized the blank ones were actually laying face-down, and they were all portraits of Jeger.

She looked over at Moreau, who had one in her hands. "Not bad," Moreau said. "The artist really captures her eyes well."

"Thanks," said a forlorn voice, and Ritchie took a step to one side to see around Blaser and Fitz. They were standing over another cadet who was sitting in the far corner, wrapped in a sleeping bag. He wasn't in uniform. He was wearing a navy blue sweatshirt with a hood that was pulled up over his head and drawn tight around his face, the bottom edge wet from what Ritchie guessed was nervous chewing. He had a paper tablet resting on his knees, and as the four of them gathered around him, he tore away a sheet of paper and tossed it aside.

Yet another lovely portrait.

Then he just looked at the blank page in front of him, his hands hanging nervelessly at his sides. If he hadn't already spoken, Ritchie might almost think he didn't know they were there.

"Vilem," he said at last. It took a moment for Ritchie to remember this was Blaser's first name. She had gotten too used to living in a world where only the last names were spoken.

"Hey, Leo," Blaser said.

"I'm sorry," Kung said, still looking at the pad of paper and not up at his buddy. "I know I promised to come back up before I was missed. I guess I probably got you in a lot of trouble?"

"Nothing I can't deal with," Blaser said.

"I'm still sorry," Kung said, and started rubbing at the pad with a stub of pencil. "I've tried, and I've tried, but I just can't get her out of my mind."

Ritchie looked around again at all the discarded portraits of Jeger. She wanted to believe Blaser that Kung could never hurt anyone, but there was no getting around that sitting in a cave drawing her over and over again was more than a little creepy.

"Are you ready to come back now?" Blaser asked.

Kung didn't answer until he had finished his drawing, torn it from the pad, and tossed it aside like all the others. Then he held the pad up for them to see that it was now empty. "I have to, I guess. I'm out of paper. And drawing on the walls would be just too crazy."

Kung started to get up, but Blaser squatted down beside him to put a hand on his shoulder. Kung gave him a puzzled look. Then Blaser looked up at the three of them. "Can we have a minute?" he asked.

"Sure," Fitz said, taking a step back. Ritchie and Moreau followed him all the way back to the entrance of the room.

Blaser spoke in a low voice close to Kung's ear. Ritchie couldn't hear his words and didn't want to openly watch Kung's reaction. But she couldn't help seeing out of the corner of her eye the way Kung's face registered shock, sort of freezing in place for several seconds. Then it started to crumple in on itself.

And there was no mistaking the sound of his sobs as he buried his face in his hands, then pressed it against his knees to cover his head with his arms, as if bracing for a bomb blast.

But it was too late to protect himself now. The damage was done.

Fitz caught Ritchie's eye and twisted his mouth in a way that said he didn't think this grief was fake. Ritchie nodded; she didn't either.

"Maybe we should go back up," Moreau whispered to them.

But Kung's sobs ended as suddenly as they had begun. He sat up, wiping at his face, then let Blaser put an arm around him to help him stand up out of the sleeping bag.

"Sorry," he said, and they all mumbled vague reassurances. He sniffled again, rubbed his cheeks and ran his hands through his hair, and then looked at them—really looked at them—for the first time. "Do I know you?"

"This is Fitz, Ritchie, and..." Blaser seemed to just then notice Moreau standing with them.

"Moreau," she supplied.

"They're sophomores," Blaser said.

"Okay. Why are they here?" Kung asked.

"We're trying to figure out who killed Jeger," Ritchie said. "Not that we thought it was you. We just heard you were close to her and hoped you might know something."

Kung gave Blaser a questioning look. "Killed? You said she died, but I thought you meant an accident."

"It was during combat flight drills," Blaser told him. "One of the gliders had a live gun on it. Apparently, not by mistake." Ritchie appreciated that he didn't mention whose glider. At least one person who wasn't a friend didn't think she had done it.

"Murder, then," Kung said darkly.

"A murder with no suspects," Ritchie said. "Can we ask you a few questions? Is that okay?"

"I've been down here since before that happened," Kung said. "What can I know that could help?"

"We're looking for anyone who might have a motive," Ritchie said.

"To be clear, you're not a suspect," Fitz added.

"Well, thanks for that," Kung said dryly.

"Leo, I'm going to pack up your stuff," Blaser said. "Do you want me to gather up the drawings?"

Kung shook his head, then turned his full attention to Ritchie and Fitz.

"I overheard an argument between Egli and Jeger the morning of the incident," Ritchie said. "Egli wanted Jeger to—I quote—'tell him or I will.' Was that about you?"

"Yeah," Kung said, looking down at his feet. "It must have been. Because Jeger met me before she went to do the prep for the combat flight drill. To tell me."

"Tell you what?" Fitz asked.

"I would've thought that was obvious," Kung said. "She told me to leave her alone."

"Were you stalking her?" Fitz asked, looking around at all the discarded portraits.

"What? No!"

"Relationships between cadets are strictly forbidden," Moreau said.

"Exactly," Kung said, giving her a nod. "Look, Jeger and I have had a flirty vibe between us since she transferred here. I like... liked her a lot." He stopped and swallowed hard before continuing. "I thought she felt the same way. In fact, I'm still sure she did. But she wasn't willing to risk her career over it. And I didn't fight her about it. I just came down here to deal with it alone. I didn't want to sit in classrooms all day processing my broken heart, you know? I don't know if you can tell, but I'm not exactly stoic."

"No," Fitz agreed. Ritchie shot him a glare.

"Egli knew," Ritchie said.

"Yes, and she insisted that Jeger end it before she got in trouble," Kung said.

"Like a good buddy would do," Moreau said.

"Blaser knew," Ritchie guessed.

"Yeah," Kung said. "And you had been talking to Egli about it before the break, right? About what you two should do if we didn't start seeing sense?"

"Yes," Blaser said, stunned. "I didn't think you knew."

Kung just shrugged.

"Did anyone else know?" Ritchie asked.

Kung looked up towards the ceiling as if scanning his memory, then shook his head. "No one."

"Is there another person caught up in this?" Fitz asked. "Like a love triangle thing?"

"Not that I know of," Kung said. "It doesn't seem likely. Most of what drew Jeger and me together was that we were... acquired tastes."

"Did she have any enemies?" Ritchie asked.

"To this extent? No way," Kung said. "This is crazy. Are we sure it wasn't just some horrific accident?"

"We're sure," Ritchie said.

Then they all went back upstairs.

16

BLASER AND KUNG walked together at the head of the group, speaking together in low voices. Moreau trailed along behind them, hands in her pockets, apparently lost in her own thoughts.

And at the tail end was Fitz with Ritchie.

"I hoped for more," he said when the silence became unbearable.

"Yeah," she said, clearly very down.

"I'm curious how Kung managed to hide down here for so long," he went on when she said no more. "Command must know this place is down here. Why didn't they just look for him here?"

"If cadets go down there in the dark of night, they already have a way of not being detected by the security systems," Ritchie said. But he could see she was thinking about how that could happen as well.

He had succeeded in distracting her. It was very clear that, on top of missing too much sleep, she was freaked out by their cave-like surroundings. She would relax when they were back in the hall with the locked storage rooms.

"I wonder how deep they go," he couldn't help saying out loud, looking back over his shoulder as they reached the beginning of the crawlspace.

"I'd rather not know," Ritchie said with a shiver. Then she took a deep breath, dropped to her hands and knees, and started crawling.

When they left all the storerooms behind and were back in the main hallway, Blaser stopped and waited for the others to cluster around him.

"I'm going to take Kung to the infirmary," he said as he pushed the plastic crate into Moreau's arms. "Can you stow this in meeting room A?"

"Sure," she said.

"Why the infirmary?" Fitz asked. Then he looked at Kung again. In the better light of the classroom hallway, he could see that Kung didn't look well. His skin was too brown for him to look exactly pale, but there was something wrong with his pallor.

"He has a fever," Blaser said. "Touch him. He radiates heat."

"I'm fine. Please don't invite people to touch me," Kung said.

"We don't have to touch you," Fitz said. "We'll take your word for it."

"Once we check in at the infirmary, Kung will no longer be considered missing," Blaser said. "I'm sorry we weren't of much use in your investigation."

"Eliminating leads is a good thing," Ritchie said in her most positive voice. But the minute they were gone, Fitz saw her deflate again. "Now we have no leads," she said glumly.

"I'm going to take this to that room," Moreau said, hoisting the crate up a bit higher in her arms.

"You got it?" Fitz asked her. She shot him a quelling look that he could just barely see over the top of the bundled sleeping bag. "It's the room with all the circuit boards in it," he told her.

"See you both at dinner, then," Moreau said.

Fitz and Ritchie stood alone in the center of the hall. Around them he could hear the murmur of voices, the sound of teachers speaking and cadets responding alone or in chorus muffled through the thick doors.

"Everyone will know he's back," Ritchie said slowly, as if piecing something together. "Everyone who didn't know he was missing will know now for sure." Then she heaved a sigh. "I sure hope no one thinks he's guilty. People don't seem to need much to go on to start throwing blame around."

"Kung is going to be fine," Fitz said. Then he started walking towards the library, Ritchie keeping pace beside him.

"I hope so," Ritchie said. "He's been through enough already. He doesn't need to be grist for the rumor mill on top of it."

"Some people don't let that sort of thing bother them at all," Fitz said. Ritchie nodded along absentmindedly. She wasn't getting him. He nudged her with his elbow. She rolled with the motion without seeming to even notice, she was so lost in her thoughts.

He nudged her again, harder.

"Ow, Fitz. What?" she demanded, rubbing at her ribs.

"I was talking about you, dummy," he said. "Every time we go into the cafeteria, you're the star of the show, but not in a good way. But you never let it bother you."

"Stars, I wish that were true," Ritchie said. "I mean the not bothering bit. It does bother me. A lot."

"Well, you don't let it show," he said.

"I guess that's a good thing," she shrugged.

They reached the library. Fitz had been hoping to sit in one of the alcoves and soak up a little natural sun after their spell deep underground. But while there were empty seats galore, there was no sun. Only steely gray clouds and rain that rattled against the windows.

"There's no point in trying to talk to Egli again," Ritchie said once they had sunken into a pair of the over-stuffed chairs. "Now that we know what that argument was about, she probably doesn't know anything more. I mean, if she had other suspicions, she would've told Moreau and me at the time."

"Agreed," Fitz said. "This might be as far as we can go. We might just have to focus on classes and let command solve the crimes." He shuddered at the thought of focusing on classes.

"Maybe that's what we should do," Ritchie said. She was rubbing at her face again. She looked bone-weary. Maybe they *should* just drop it. He knew Ritchie didn't do it. Soon everyone else would as well.

But he couldn't. He didn't have that kind of faith in the system. And sitting around waiting really wasn't his style.

"There's Keller and Wyss and what they're working on," he said.

Ritchie drew her lips into a tight line. She nodded, but it wasn't an enthusiastic gesture.

"You don't think they'll find anything?" he guessed.

"No, they might," she said. "They're both super smart. Given enough time and resources, I wouldn't want to bet against them doing anything they put their minds to."

"But?" he prompted.

"Ugh," Ritchie said, rubbing at her forehead. "I guess it's no secret that Keller bugs me."

"No," he said slowly. "It's also no secret that she's the source of that problem. Not you."

"I just don't like talking about my dad," Ritchie said. She was looking out the window at the rain, and she was blinking a lot.

"I know," Fitz said. There was no way he could say it out loud, but if there was anyone that wanted to talk about her dad less than Ritchie, it was Fitz.

"I know it was a long time ago," Ritchie said.

"Not really," Fitz said. "At least, it doesn't feel that long ago to me."

She glanced at him for the briefest of moments, then looked out the window again. He had no idea what that look had meant.

"I mean, it feels like we were apart for an eternity," he said. "That part feels like forever. But the part about... what happened, it feels like that was just yesterday."

"It feels the same for me," Ritchie said. "It's ancient history, but it's still so raw."

"She shouldn't be dredging that up," Fitz said.

"Well," Ritchie said. "I mean, I can see why she does. She has really good questions. And she has good reasons for asking those questions. I get it. It's just... I can't summon up the answers."

"That's not what you're here for," Fitz said. "To be pumped for answers about your dad? No."

"She's not out of line," Ritchie insisted. "It's relevant to what she's studying."

"No," Fitz said firmly. "It's relevant to what she wants to study later. That's way beyond the scope of this academy. She's nearly four years away from that level of study. More, actually. That level of work is beyond the first four years of diplomat training as well."

"I'm hardly going to fault her for wanting to work ahead," Ritchie said almost defensively.

"Hey, it's different when it's you," Fitz said. Ritchie just scoffed, but he was undeterred. "It *is* different. You're handling your advanced studies on your own. You're not pestering others to pull you ahead."

"I'm not sure if that's exactly what she's doing," Ritchie said. She was quiet for a moment, just watching the rain. "Maybe I should try to be nicer to her."

"What, encourage her?" Fitz said lightheartedly. Then more seriously, "do you worry it will be like that with everyone in diplomat school?"

Ritchie gave him a surprised look. "Why do you assume I'll be in diplomat school?"

Fitz didn't know how to respond to that. It had been such a natural assumption. He had never once thought she might be planning for a guardian career.

"Is it because of my dad?" she asked, and there was a dangerous edge to her voice.

"No," he said. "I mean, a little, right? But, Murdina, I remember you from back then. You loved helping your dad. More than that, you were good at it. Why wouldn't you stick with it?"

"Because I don't think it's for me," Ritchie said. She was looking out the window again, but this time he was sure she was blinking because she was fighting back tears.

Guilt squeezed at his heart. Couldn't he have left it alone? Here he was annoyed with Keller for dredging all this up when Keller wasn't capable of upsetting Ritchie anywhere near the way Fitz could. She might know everything there was to know about Ritchie's dad and his work, but Fitz knew Murdina Ritchie.

She was meant to be a diplomat. And not just because of her skill with alien communication, a strange knack for intention and meaning so developed that by the age of ten her father, with all of his years of schooling and practice in the field, still listened to what she had to say.

She also had compassion, a sense of fairness, a way of bringing people together.

But what happened with her father was pulling her away from trusting her communication skills. And Fitz was starting to suspect that being apart from others at the academy was taking a toll on her people skills.

He had to fix this for her. He owed it to her.

"Look, let's go find Keller and Wyss and see what they have," he said, sitting forward in his chair, hands on knees, ready to get to his feet. "If Keller starts in on anything, I'll nip it in the bud. I'll be like a shield between you."

"Thanks, but it's really okay," Ritchie said. "I can deal with her on my own."

"Just because you *can* do something doesn't mean it should always be on you to *do* it," he said. "Come on. I can see you haven't slept much in the last two nights. And it's not even lunchtime yet. It's going to be a long day, no matter what happens. Let me do this much for you."

"Fine," Ritchie said. "If it comes up, have at her."

Fitz couldn't stop the grin from spreading across his face if he tried. They both got to their feet and headed towards the meeting rooms at the back of the library.

"Oh, and Fitz?" Ritchie said.

"Yes?"

"Don't call me Murdina."

Had he? Had that slipped out of his mouth? "Of course not. Very inappropriate between cadets. Sorry."

17

KELLER AND WYSS'S usual meeting room had its walls once more set to opaque. Fitz knocked once, then just opened the door, and he and Ritchie both slipped inside.

It was, as usual, dark. They could see Keller's and Wyss's faces lit up by the holographic screen of the tabletop. Moreau was there as well, standing just behind them, her pale face lit more dramatically from below. All three looked up when Ritchie and Fitz came in.

At first, Ritchie thought they surely must have good news. They were all leaning so intently over the tabletop, and there was a feeling in the air like their arrival had interrupted a moment of close conversation. But then Moreau straightened up, and the lighting on her face changed, becoming less a dramatic show of light and shadow, her expression more plainly visible.

When they had first met, Ritchie had found Moreau's face maddeningly unreadable. But over the time they had spent together as roommates and buddies, Ritchie had learned the little changes in the set of her mouth or where she looked with her eyes that gave away her actual moods. They were subtle, but she had gotten good at sensing them.

None of those skills were necessary just now. Moreau was biting her lip. There was a deep furrow between her brows. Her jaw was held so tight Ritchie could see the little muscle in her temple twitching.

"What is it?" Ritchie asked, trying to see what was being displayed on the tabletop. But it was all text, upside-down to her on the wrong side of the table.

"It's the program," Moreau said, but then she just threw up her hands. "Maybe Wyss had better explain." She crossed her arms and turned away, melting into the shadows at the back of the room.

Ritchie gave Wyss a questioning look.

"I was running a program," Wyss said. "We know someone made changes both to the laser cannon and the glider itself, right?"

"Because the firing mechanism was connected when it shouldn't have been," Fitz said.

"Exactly," Wyss said. "So I created a program to compare all the surveillance of the glider and all the surveillance of the laser cannon itself. It was creating a list of any person who showed up in both feeds. It was going to give us a starting point, a list of suspects to start narrowing down."

"Perfect," Ritchie said. "But?"

"The program crashed," Wyss said. "It was nearly done, but I didn't look at any of the names it had compiled yet. I was just going to wait until it was all done. But then it crashed, and it's all gone."

"The names?" Ritchie asked.

"Everything," Wyss said. He sounded choked up about it, even more upset than Moreau. Which seemed like an outsized reaction from both of them.

"Can't you just fix it and start it again?" Fitz asked. "I'd think it'd go even faster the second time around. Assuming you caught the mistake you made the first time, I mean."

"I don't just mean the names and the program are gone," Wyss said. "It's everything."

Ritchie's stomach sank. None of this sounded good. Wyss buried his face in his hands and sat quietly. Keller beside him looked like she wanted to burst into tears.

"Can *you* explain?" Ritchie asked her gently.

"It's my fault," Keller said.

"No, it isn't," Wyss said, his voice muffled by his hands.

"It is," she insisted. "Wyss wanted to duplicate all the surveillance videos first, to make a copy on our own server instead of running his program with the original files on the academy security systems server."

Ritchie's stomach knotted up tighter and sank a little lower. She was starting to understand.

"Why didn't you?" Fitz asked.

"Because I said it would be faster to just run it from the originals," Keller said. "It was faster. And the risk seemed so ridiculously low. Wyss's programs are fool-proof, always."

Wyss dropped his hands from his face and started scanning through the text screen in front of him again, his expression grimly determined. "Not this time," he said.

"You'll find the error," Fitz said confidently. "We can try again."

"No, we can't," Keller said. "When the program crashed, it corrupted every file it was touching."

"Which was every surveillance file that showed the glider and the gun," Wyss said. "They're all gone now. We can't try again. There's nothing left to try it on."

"We didn't have permission to access those files, obviously," Moreau said from the shadows. "And now that they've been corrupted, command can't access them either."

"So we've basically crashed our own little investigation and the official one both at once," Fitz said and gave a low whistle. "I have a feeling we're going to get into real trouble for that."

"I'm so sorry!" Keller said, clearly fighting a losing battle against those oncoming tears.

"I'll go confess," Wyss said grimly. "It was my program. They'll recognize my work anyway, so there's no reason not to. And that way, the rest of you are safe."

"They'll expel you," Fitz said. Wyss just gave a shrug that convinced none of them that he didn't care.

"I should go now," he said. "Get it over with."

"Wait," Ritchie said, stepping between him and the door. "Are you *sure* you can't fix this?"

"I'm sure," he said, not meeting her eyes. "My only real hope is that, unlike me, command made a copy."

"Yes," Fitz said. "They must have a backup. That's got to be protocol."

"I already checked," Keller said. "The backup was running when the program crashed. It was corrupted, too."

"How could this all have gone so catastrophically wrong at just the worst moment?" Ritchie asked.

"I'm going," Wyss said. "It's the best thing for everybody."

"I don't think—" Ritchie started to say, but he just pushed past her and ran out of the room.

"Wyss!" Keller cried, propelling herself out of her chair to run after him. "I'll stop him!" she shouted back to them just before the door shut behind her.

Moreau stepped closer to the light from the table, touching first Wyss's display screen and then Keller's. But she didn't seem to be looking for anything in particular. She was just fidgeting.

"I don't suppose you saw any of the names before it crashed?" Fitz asked hopefully.

"No," Moreau said. "When I came in, they had just discovered the program had stopped. Then they discovered they had corrupted all the files."

"Can't we reset the computer back fifteen minutes or something? There must be something," Fitz said.

Moreau let out a long exhale. "Well, look at this," she said, turning Wyss's screen around and pushing it across the tabletop towards them. "I don't know much about computer programs, but this sort of epic fail all at once? I've never seen anything like it."

Ritchie looked at the log screen. She didn't know any more than Moreau did, but her gut also found it all too fishy. "I meant what I said before. I wasn't being rhetorical or exaggerating or anything. How could this all have gone so catastrophically wrong at just the worst moment?"

"You're saying it wasn't an accident?" Fitz asked her.

"Just like my gun suddenly being armed and the firing mechanism in my glider being attached wasn't an accident," Ritchie said.

"So someone did this," Moreau said. "I'm sure Wyss can figure it out as soon as he stops beating himself up for it even happening in the first place."

"Assuming he gets a chance to," Fitz said.

"Yeah, I'm going to go help Keller bring him back here," Moreau said, then brushed past them to go out the door.

Ritchie and Fitz looked over the logs one more time but learned nothing new. They really needed Wyss.

"Maybe I should confess," Ritchie said.

"Confess to what?" Fitz asked.

"To running my own unauthorized investigation," Ritchie said. "I have a history of it, after all."

"We both do," Fitz said. "But what would be the point of confessing to that?"

"Command should know as soon as possible that their files have been corrupted, don't you think?" she said.

"They'll know soon enough," Fitz said. "There's nothing they can do right now they won't be able to do later when they do discover it."

"Okay," Ritchie said. "But maybe we can avoid expulsion by being honest."

"How's that?" Fitz asked.

"They'll go easier on us because we showed integrity?" Ritchie said. She wasn't sure if she believed it.

Fitz, on the other hand, appeared absolutely certain that he didn't. He scoffed then said, "they only tell you that because it makes their jobs easier if they can convince cadets to confess to everything."

"How do you know?" Ritchie asked. "You're always so cynical. Have you ever tried admitting you were wrong and seeing how that went for you?"

"Yes, actually," Fitz said. "I've been expelled from a lot of schools, Ritchie."

"So you keep telling me," Ritchie said.

"Some of those expulsions were for things I did that I didn't admit guilt to, sure. And some were for things I didn't do; I was just the likely suspect. I've occasionally admitted I was guilty when I was. I've even once taken the blame for something I didn't do."

"Why would you do that?" Ritchie asked, shocked.

"A story for another time," he said with a dismissive wave. "The point was—"

"That the punishment was always the same," Ritchie interrupted. "Expulsion. So, where does that leave us now?"

"The best-case scenario is that we get Wyss back in here and help him in any way we can to fix this," Fitz said. "If we can fix things before anyone notices they're broken, yay for us."

"I don't want to bank all my hopes on a best-case scenario," Ritchie said.

"No, me neither," Fitz said. "Which is why I really advocate for Plan B."

"What's Plan B?" Ritchie asked.

"Having the name of the real killer all ready to go by the time they figure out that we're the ones that corrupted all those files," Fitz said.

"I like Plan B," Ritchie said. "There's just one problem."

"I know," Fitz sighed, then tried to muster up an encouraging grin. "You think the lack of any leads is going to hamper us."

"Yeah, just a bit," Ritchie said, refusing to let him cheer her.

Well, refusing to let him see that he had cheered her. That grin was infectious. Still, it was all so impossible. But it was all they had.

"Let's go get Wyss back in here," she said.

18

FITZ LET Ritchie take the lead as they crossed the library towards the main hallway and the administrative wing.

If she couldn't see his face, then he could let himself relax for a moment. Not for a minute did he think they were going to find a way out of this, but he couldn't let her see that. He needed her focused on solving the crime while he dealt with how he was going to manage to keep her from getting expelled.

And to think that thought had been niggling in his mind even before she decided she should throw herself on her sword for the sake of the others.

Fitz certainly didn't merit it. He knew that. He also knew his dad had been serious. If he got expelled, he'd be enlisted the next day in some military branch's lowest ranks. He wouldn't be a guardian; he'd be a soldier. But he had had enough time to sit with that possibility. It no longer scared him. It wasn't his first choice, but he'd handle it if that's how things shook out.

He didn't know about Keller and Wyss, what their personal stories were. But he knew they were both staggeringly bright. He wasn't even sure why they had taken on a foreign service education, of all things. If they were expelled, they were unlikely to be taken by another academy. Neither of them had a father like he had. But he was sure they'd have no problem getting into any science or technology program at any university in the Union of Free Worlds. They might even be happier there. They would fit in better, for sure.

But Ritchie?

Well, he couldn't imagine anywhere where Ritchie wouldn't succeed. When she put her mind to it, she could accomplish pretty much anything. Which was why it was so maddening that she had barely been accepted at this, the lowest rung of foreign service academies, and even that as a late entry, probationary student. If she were expelled, her foreign service career would be over before it ever started.

Fitz couldn't let that happen. The Union of Free Worlds needed her. Even if they were too dumb to know it yet.

The two of them reached the point where the corridor to the administrative wing crossed the main hall and found Wyss trying to push his way past Moreau and Keller. He wasn't a big guy, but they were both tiny as well. Fitz ran up behind him and caught him by the collar.

"Here," Ritchie said, running to open the door to the room where Blaser had been doing his circuit board checking punishment. The table was still covered with mountains of boards, but there was no sign of Blaser.

Fitz pushed Wyss down into a chair as Keller and Moreau came in behind him. Ritchie looked up and down the hall to see if anyone had noticed them, then gave Fitz a little shake of her head before closing the door.

"Listen, this wasn't your mistake," Fitz said to Wyss. "So there's nothing for you to confess."

"It doesn't matter why the program failed," Wyss said. "It matters that I made the choice to touch all the live files. The fact that they are corrupted is on me. It's absolutely my mistake."

"It was my idea, though," Keller said.

"It was my call," Wyss said, not looking at her. "It was a bad call."

"The thing is," Fitz said, leaning in until Wyss finally met his eyes, "we're pretty sure it was sabotage."

"Like with Ritchie's glider," Moreau added.

"That means the real killer is aware of what we're doing," Ritchie said as if she had just thought of it.

"But who could know?" Wyss asked. "We keep that room on lockdown."

"I walked right in," Fitz said.

"Yeah, because we were in there, and we knew it was you," Wyss said. "You didn't really think all I had done to keep anyone else out was to opaque the walls?"

Fitz had actually thought just that. "It's possible you're a bit paranoid."

"And yet, someone got in," Wyss said, crossing his arms. "So, not paranoid enough."

"Look," Fitz said, sweeping his gaze around the entire room to be sure he had everyone's attention. "No one is going to confess to anything. That's crazy talk. We're going to figure this out. We're going to find the killer."

"Oh!" Keller said, and Fitz could swear her frizzy red hair suddenly stood up higher on her head.

"What is it?" Ritchie asked.

"The room," she said, already moving towards the door. "We left it open."

Ritchie swore, then threw open the door. Keller ran back towards the library, but Ritchie stopped to look back at Fitz. He gave her a little thumbs-up, and she returned the signal before running after Keller. Moreau crossed the room to close the door, then turned back to Fitz and Wyss.

"The first thing we need to know is how much time do you think we have? How long before someone notices the corrupted files?" Fitz asked.

"If they're working the case, I don't know how they don't know already," Wyss said.

"But clearly they don't," Fitz said, "or we would've heard from them already. So best-case scenario: they did everything they needed to with those files before they were corrupted. They aren't going to need them for the case again. In that scenario, how long until someone notices?"

"The backup was corrupted as well," Wyss said slowly as he

thought it through. "They'll notice for sure when the backup runs again, and the files don't match. It will generate an error."

"Do you know when that is?" Fitz asked.

"Not specifically, but sometime in the early morning. Those are the most off-peak hours, avoiding both the late studiers and the early risers who might be on the system. Say three or four in the morning?"

"Okay, we'll use that as a benchmark for our ticking clock," Fitz said. "That's how much time you have."

"To do what?" Wyss asked. "I think I've messed up your investigation more than enough already."

"No—" Fitz started to say, but then he felt Moreau rest her arm on his shoulder, and he fell silent.

"We need you, Wyss," Moreau said, and Wyss's cheeks pinkened ever so slightly. "You're the only one who can figure out who tampered with your program."

"And whoever tampered with your program is either the killer or an accomplice," Fitz said.

"I guess I can do that," Wyss said. "I was so shocked when I saw that it had failed, and then that everything else had been corrupted, I never even started trying to get to the bottom of what went wrong."

"Solving this case is the best thing for all of us," Moreau said. "Command really wants us to show we can police ourselves."

"Sure, when it comes to keeping the barracks clean and performing our assigned duties. But this? This is murder," Wyss said.

"Still," Fitz said with a shrug. "I think she's right. For all we know, they already know who did it. They're just waiting to see if we can figure it out."

"That's evil," Wyss said vehemently.

"We're training to be officers," Moreau said. "We'll have responsibilities. Even as raw lieutenants, we may be in situations with dozens of soldiers under our command while we're isolated from our own superiors. Rookies behind enemy lines, nothing to rely on but ourselves and our training. We don't think about that much—the Union of Free Worlds has been at peace since long before we were born—but that doesn't mean we should assume it could never happen."

Fitz tried to catch her eye and throw her a questioning eyebrow, but her gaze never wavered from Wyss. When this was all over, he definitely had to talk to her and Ritchie. Why was everyone talking like a war was on the way? What was he missing?

"Being a lieutenant is six years or more in my future," Wyss said.

"But you're meant to be preparing for it now," Moreau said.

Wyss looked to Fitz, who just shrugged. "That's part of foreign service. Potentially."

"So what happens in the morning if we haven't solved this?" Wyss asked.

"You don't even have to wonder," Fitz said, putting out a hand to pull Wyss to his feet, "because that's not going to happen. Because you're going to help us get to the bottom of this. Between now and dawn? That's plenty of time."

"Maybe," Wyss said. He didn't sound convinced, but when Moreau opened the door to let him out into the hall, he was already mumbling to himself, his fingers twitching as if he were enumerating a list in his own mind.

"Do you really think they know?" Moreau whispered to Fitz as he joined her outside the door.

"No," Fitz said. "But I agree with you. This is on us to solve. If anything command was doing was having any kind of result, we'd know who the culprit was already."

"They must be good, whoever did this," Moreau said. "Not morally. I meant competent."

"Wicked competent," Fitz said with a wry grin.

"Not only did they leave no real evidence, they're removing what evidence we can find before we can even see it," she went on. "How did they know what Wyss was doing?"

"Maybe they're smarter than Wyss," Fitz said. "He and Keller are smart, but not inhumanly so. Maybe we should search school records for someone particularly good at this sort of thing."

"I don't know what we'd be looking for. We have no classes in getting away with murder," Moreau said.

19

RITCHIE HAD NEVER BEEN the type to cram a bunch of studying in the night before a big test. Not that she was opposed to doing a ton of work, she just never left it until the end. A manageable amount every day was better than pulling an all-nighter. That was always her way.

But now here she was, sitting in a library studying room with four others, trying to make sense of what was written on a holographically projected board when it was closer to sunrise than sunset.

Clearly, her body hated staying up all night. Her eyes were hot and dry and reluctant to focus, her entire body ached no matter how she shifted around in her chair, and her mouth tasted like something had died in it.

Plowing through a deliberately sleepless night on top of two mostly sleepless nights had probably not been a great idea. But there hadn't been anything else she could do. And now here she was, totally wrecked, but with nothing to show for it.

"Okay, we've been staring at this without talking for half an hour," Fitz said, pushing himself to his feet. "I'm going to get more coffee and some egg sandwiches."

Moreau, who was sitting across from Ritchie with her eyes closed as if in a deep sleep, said, "I'll go with you."

"We're almost out of time," Ritchie said.

"We're probably already out of time," Fitz said, rubbing at the back of his head. "That's no reason to quit."

"But you're leaving," she said.

"Only to get more fuel," he said. "We'll just be a second."

The two of them slipped out of the door. The library outside was still mostly dark, lit only by the bluish lights that marked out the walking areas across the floor. Ritchie tried to turn her attention back to the list of names, but the letters just danced in front of her eyes.

"How is it going with you two?" she asked, turning towards Wyss and Keller. They weren't working together at the moment. Wyss was using half of the holographic table to hunt through every line of code in his program, but Keller was working on the smaller computer work-station in the corner.

"Nothing so far," Wyss said without looking up. "Whoever did this was very good at covering up their tracks."

"In lots of ways," Ritchie sighed. "How about you, Keller?"

Keller pushed away from her workstation and stood up to stretch. "So far, I see no sign of any uncorrupted backups anywhere in the academy systems. But I can tell someone accessed them from a remote device, like a tablet. If they switched that tablet off after, it might still be in its cache."

"Not likely," Wyss scoffed. "Who switches a tablet off?"

Ritchie couldn't remember turning any of her own devices off, ever. As far as she knew, it only needed to be done if someone intended to touch the hardware, like for a repair.

"We might get lucky," she said. "Do you have any idea whose tablet it was?"

"Nope," Keller said, rolling her weight from her heels to her toes and swinging her arms. "But I will in a bit, I'm sure."

"That's something, I guess," Ritchie said.

The door opened, and the air was immediately filled with the rich smell of fresh coffee, fried eggs, and melted cheese.

"How do you do it?" Wyss asked, shaking his head as he reached for one of the sandwiches on the plate Fitz held out to him.

"I have my ways," Fitz said. "And no use asking Moreau. I've sworn her to secrecy."

"He has," Moreau agreed as she handed out the coffees. They ate quickly but in a companionable silence, then turned back to their separate tasks, still sipping at the huge mugs of coffee.

"I don't think our suspect list is of any use at all," Fitz said when Ritchie switched the holographic board back on. "We've basically only eliminated ourselves and, like, three other people."

"Agreed," Ritchie said. The coffee was waking up her brain, but she knew the effect would be short-lived. Then she'd be crashing twice as hard as before. She had to figure this all out before that happened. She looked across the table at Fitz. "I want to look at the glider."

"Ooh," Moreau said over the rim of her coffee mug. "Really?"

"Why not?" Ritchie asked. They were all frowning at her.

"The entire hangar deck was locked down as a crime scene," Fitz told her. "I thought you knew."

"That must have happened when I was in the brig," she said. "Yeah, I guess Bale mentioned that. But so what? We break one more rule. Does that change anything at this point?"

"It might, actually," Fitz said. Ritchie never thought she'd see Fitz be the one worried about breaking the rules.

"Do you really think you'll see anything now that you didn't see before?" Moreau asked. She sounded worried, too.

"Maybe," Ritchie said. "I guess I won't know until I either do or don't. Why are you all so shocked by this suggestion?"

"It's a crime scene," Fitz said. "If you thought corrupting the files was bad, just imagine what we could do to the physical evidence."

"But they will have already collected all of that, right?" Ritchie said. She rubbed at the spot just at the top of the bridge of her nose, where a tiny headache was starting to coalesce. "Look, we're not doing any good here. I don't see what else we can do. I'm exhausted, but I know there's no chance at all that I will get any sleep even if I tried. So what else is there? I want to look at the glider again. I need to be sure I didn't miss anything."

The room was quiet for a long moment. Then Fitz clapped his

hands down on the tabletop and pushed himself back to his feet. "All right, then. Let's go."

"I'll go, too," Moreau said and finished off the last of her coffee.

"Are you sure?" Ritchie asked. "We can do it if you're not up for it."

"I'm up for it," Moreau said, but didn't exactly sound enthused. "If you get caught, I might as well get caught with you. I'd rather get in trouble for that than for not knowing what my buddy is up to."

"You guys keep working on what you're working on," Fitz said to Wyss and Keller. "We'll be back."

"Sure you will," Wyss said drily without looking up. Keller just gave them a little wave over her shoulder.

The sky outside the library windows was only just lightening up to a steely gray. At least it wasn't raining at the moment. They pushed through both sets of doors and out into the cold wind.

"Maybe we should go back for our coats?" Moreau said, already visibly shivering.

"No, let's just run for it," Ritchie said.

It was a long way to run, especially on so little sleep, but the icy bite of the wind was a strong motivator. Fitz reached the far side first, disappearing down the hallway that sloped down to the hangar deck. Moreau was keeping pace by Ritchie's side, although Ritchie was pretty sure she could've kept up with Fitz if she had wanted. But Moreau took the buddy thing pretty seriously.

They slowed to a walk when they reached the hallway and were out of the wind, although the air was still bone-chilling all on its own. Then Fitz lunged up out of the darkness ahead of them.

"Sorry," he said when they both jumped. "No guards, though. That's a good thing."

They walked down to the hangar deck, where the lights were still on from Fitz's first trip down. Ritchie couldn't see her glider from the bottom of the hallway, but she could see where it was parked. That entire bay was closed off by long sheets of plastic.

"They didn't move it," she said. When Fitz and Moreau both turned to look at her, she added, "I was afraid they might have."

"And yet you wanted to come," Fitz said, raising one eyebrow.

"Let's go see what there is to see and get back," Moreau said. Her hands were buried deep in her pockets, and she was still shivering.

"You're anxious to go back out into that?" Fitz asked.

"It's warmer in the library than it is in here," she said. Which was true.

"Okay, let's go," Ritchie said, leading the way across the deck and through a break in the curtain. The glider stood there, as golden and beautiful as ever, but the gun was gone. "Oh," she said, completely failing to hide the disappointment in her voice.

"The gun?" Fitz guessed. "Look, it's just over there." Ritchie followed where he was pointing towards the hangar wall just beyond the nose of her glider. A cart the size of a dining room table was parked there, and on top of the cart was the laser cannon from her glider.

"Of course they took it all apart," Ritchie said. "I should've guessed."

"That doesn't mean there's nothing to learn here," Fitz said. "We came all this way."

Ritchie nodded, and the two of them walked up to the cart to get a closer look. She didn't realize that the warm feeling in her chest had been a glimmer of hope until just now, when it died away.

The three of them stood over the disassembled pieces of the gun for some time before Fitz finally made the first move, picking up part of the firing mechanism to examine it under the harsh hangar deck light.

"Oh, look," Moreau said, picking something else up. Or rather several somethings that jangled together across the palm of her hand. "Mini drones."

"Wyss and Keller?" Ritchie guessed.

Moreau picked one up between her thumb and forefinger to take a closer look. To Ritchie's eye, they just looked like so many metallic disks, like really thick coins, but judging from Moreau's studious frown, she saw more.

"I don't think so," she said slowly as she turned it to a different angle in the light. "Wyss puts a little mark on all of his. Like his own logo. I don't know what it's supposed to be, looks like a smudge to me, but it's always the same shade of red. These don't have that."

"Look," Fitz said. He was holding the cannon and staring down the barrel, an image that made Ritchie jump. She knew it wasn't a live gun, but then she had assumed that about this exact gun before.

"What?" Moreau asked, trying to look over his shoulder down the barrel.

"Those scrapes on the sides. Do you see them? Have your implant magnify your vision, and you will," he said.

"Oh," Moreau said.

"What is it?" Ritchie asked. She really didn't want to look for herself. With her recent luck, that could turn ugly fast.

"It looks like they found these drones inside the gun," Moreau said. She stepped closer to Ritchie until Ritchie could see the little disk in Moreau's fingers had little spindly legs coming out of it. "They were crawling around the inside. I don't think these can even fly at all."

"So definitely not Wyss' work then," Ritchie said. "This is how it was sabotaged?"

"This is how they sabotaged *the gun*," Fitz specified as he set the gun back down on the cart. Then he looked back over his shoulder at the glider. "Actually, maybe the gun and the glider both."

"How?" Ritchie asked.

"Say someone put these little guys inside the gun while it was in storage in the battery," Fitz said. "Just four little guys, and they could look like part of the mechanism to the untrained eye, right?"

"Especially if they were inside and not visible to the outside," Ritchie said. "If they weren't moving."

"Hiding, lurking, waiting," Moreau said.

"Until just the right moment," Fitz said. "Then they crawl around inside the gun, activating the firing capability."

"Can they do that?" Ritchie asked, looking at the tiny disk in Moreau's hand again. "With those little spindly things?"

"I should have Wyss show you his," Moreau said. "But I'd say yes. Those spindly things can telescope out, branch into extensions, manipulate things with more precision than my little fingers."

"But the gun alone wasn't enough," Ritchie said.

"Exactly," Fitz said. "So they crawled outside of the gun, over the surface of the glider, until they found the port where the wiring is supposed to run that connects the trigger in the yoke to the firing mechanism. And they rewired it."

"But only just before I shot Jeger," Ritchie said. "Not when I was flying through the rest of the mission, pretending to shoot down a bunch of other cadets. So there are two possibilities. One, that it just took that long for them to accomplish their task. Or two, someone was watching and remotely triggered them after only three of us were still up there."

"I'm thinking it was two," Fitz said.

"But Wyss and Keller already tried to find evidence of anyone using a remote trigger, and there wasn't one," Moreau said.

"Maybe the programming in these things is just that sophisticated?" Fitz said.

"Or maybe the evidence they were looking for had already been removed from their own drone data by our saboteur," Moreau said. "I'm still voting for the trigger thing. Someone was watching you, Ritchie. Watching and waiting for the perfect moment."

"Oh my stars," Ritchie said, putting a hand over her mouth. Fitz just drew his eyebrows together in confusion. His brain hadn't leaped to the same conclusion as hers. "You were up there too. And you were on Jeger's team. It could just as likely have been you as her. I could've killed you."

"No," Moreau said. "None of this was left to chance. If you had taken a shot at Fitz, it would've just been counted as a holographic kill, the same as the others."

"If whoever did this was actually trying to kill Jeger," Ritchie said. "What if all they wanted was to frame me for a murder? Anyone's murder?"

"Who would do that?" Fitz asked in what was clearly meant to be a joking manner. But Ritchie couldn't think of it as all a joke.

"We should go to the battery," Ritchie said. "I want to be sure mine was the only gun tampered with. And maybe there are clues there as well. More of the little drones or something."

"I'm sure command has already done all that," Fitz said.

"Well, I'm doing it again," Ritchie said. She knew she sounded beyond grumpy, but the headache that had been building in the center of her forehead was now a tight, painful band behind her eyes. And still growing.

"I'll go with Ritchie," Moreau said. "Fitz, you should get back to Wyss and Keller."

"But—" Fitz started to say.

"Do it," Moreau said firmly. Ritchie had a hand pressed to her eyes so she couldn't see what was passing between them, but she knew something was. "If everything goes sideways now that it's morning, they're going to need you with them. You can talk your way out of anything. That's definitely not in either of their skill sets."

"You'll be coming back after you check the battery, right?" he asked.

"One way or another," Ritchie said, still pressing her hand to her head. "One way or another, this will all be over soon."

20

FITZ WASN'T PARTICULARLY adept at picking up on nonverbal communication at the best of times, and dawn after a sleepless night was far from the best of times. But even if he had that particular skill, he knew Moreau would be a tough read. Ritchie herself had complained about it on occasion.

So that look in Moreau's eyes when she had told him to get back to Wyss and Keller? He wasn't sure if it was a plea or a command, but he knew what she wanted. She wanted time alone with Ritchie.

Which annoyed him. What could they possibly have to say or do that couldn't include Fitz?

Buddy stuff.

So the one who wasn't a buddy—who didn't even have a buddy—had to go.

Running back through the cold wind to the library did little to improve his mood. But he had to admit, Moreau was right about one thing. When doom fell upon them, Keller and Wyss could not be left alone to face it. They needed him.

He jogged along the row of glass-walled study spaces until he got to the last one, the one whose walls were pretty much always set to opaque now. He pushed open the door without knocking first, a greeting and query all ready to go.

But they died unspoken as he stepped into harshly bright light. The holograms were all gone from the tabletop, and the spare workstation was shut down. Keller wasn't there; her chair wasn't even pulled up to that workstation anymore. All the chairs were arranged around the table, neatly stowed.

All except one, the one Wyss had been using. But it wasn't Wyss in it, waiting patiently with his hands folded across his stomach.

No, it was Colonel Hansen.

"Colonel?" Fitz said, then remembered himself well enough to snap to attention and salute.

"At ease, cadet," Hansen said. He sounded amused. Why did he sound amused?

"Where are Keller and Wyss?" Fitz asked, then regretted it. If they had been gone before Hansen came in, he had just given them away. He cursed the lack of sleep dulling his wits, plus the excess of coffee that was making him too quick to talk.

"I sent them down to the barracks," Hansen said.

"Oh," Fitz said, relieved both that he hadn't just said their names when he shouldn't have and that they weren't currently in detention.

"To shower and get ready for classes," Hansen went on as if Fitz hadn't spoken. "No rest for the wicked."

"The wicked," Fitz repeated. Hansen just sat as patiently as ever, hands folded as he watched Fitz struggle to find words. "Um, why are you here, sir?"

"Why do you think I'm here?" Hansen asked.

Fitz swallowed hard. He could stick to a story—say, that they were up all night studying together for some reason—but without knowing what Keller and Wyss might have said, that plan was doomed to fail. "You found out that we corrupted the video surveillance files," he said instead.

"'We?' That's good to know," Hansen said. "Wyss said he was acting alone, but that didn't really feel like the truth."

"No, he was doing me a favor," Fitz said.

"Just you?"

Fitz clenched his jaw to keep his mouth shut. On the one hand, honesty was the best policy. Not as a general rule, of course, but he could reasonably assume that if he wanted to match Wyss's story, he would have to tell the truth.

But on the other hand, he was incapable of implicating Ritchie in anything. He just couldn't do it.

"I asked him to look into what happened with Ritchie's glider and the gun," Fitz said. "I know she didn't do it, sir."

"Technically, she did," Hansen said. "But we all know it was an act of sabotage. There was no need for you to rope other cadets into skipping classes, neglecting disciplinary duties, infiltrating off-limits sections of the academy, and violating curfew. Especially novice cadets."

"Wyss and Keller aren't like other novice cadets," Fitz said.

"That's not the point."

"No, sir," Fitz said. He desperately wanted to ask which off-limits parts of the academy the colonel was referring to: the subbasements or the hangar? Or the gun battery, where Moreau and Ritchie should be right at that moment?

"You do realize you are on disciplinary probation, cadet?"

"Yes, sir," Fitz said. "I'm on thin ice. I know it."

"And yet, all this?"

"It felt more important at the time," Fitz said. As hard as Moreau was to read, Hansen was even harder. Perhaps it was the scar tissue left behind after whatever had happened to his face. His expression was always blandly neutral. What was he thinking? Was he angry? Disappointed? Just there to do the job of telling Fitz he was expelled?

"And now?" Hansen asked.

"It still feels important," Fitz said.

"So, you think there's a murderer on the loose, and only you can find them?" Hansen asked.

"No," Fitz said.

"Well, as it happens, there is a murderer on the loose," Hansen said, to Fitz's complete surprise. "And they've covered their tracks very, very well."

"Oh," Fitz said, too shocked to find better words. "But you don't mean the rest too, do you? That I'm supposed to find them?"

"Obviously not, cadet," Hansen said with a sound that might have been a chuckle. "We on the faculty have done all we could, but we're not experts. The experts will be here sometime this afternoon or evening, depending, as always, on the weather."

"But the corrupted files—" Fitz started to say.

"There are backups," Hansen said. "They are off the main system. Quite safe. Although it seems like young Cadet Keller had almost figured out where they were. She's quite clever. But in this matter, she's shown a tenacity that's lacking in her classroom work. Thoughts?"

"Oh," Fitz said, caught off guard by the random question. "Thoughts about Keller? Well, I do know she's bored in her classes. She complains about that a lot." Hansen nodded. But then another thought occurred to Fitz. "She's also quite fond of Ritchie personally."

"Is that so?" Hansen asked.

"She's interested in communication, particularly among aliens who use nonverbal communication, either primarily or exclusively," Fitz said. When Hansen still didn't seem to understand, he added, "that was Ritchie's father's specialty."

"Oh, of course," Hansen said. "You're right. I had quite forgotten."

"So you're pretty confident this murderer isn't planning to strike again, I take it?" Fitz said.

"Why do you conclude that?" Hansen asked, back in inscrutable instructor mode.

"Because the academy isn't in lockdown?"

"We haven't stopped classes," Hansen said. "But combat drills are all modified. You would know that if you hadn't skipped your hand-to-hand class yesterday."

"You think the murderer is going to kill someone else, but with their bare hands?" Fitz asked.

Hansen narrowed his eyes in a look Fitz knew all too well. His humor was so seldom appreciated by the officers. "We're taking no chances."

Fitz was tempted to argue that point, but then he realized that as much as Hansen knew everything he had been up to in the last few days, command probably knew the same about every single cadet.

He knew Blaser hadn't been paranoid about feeling like they were being watched. But it still gave him a prickly, uncomfortable feeling.

"You knew we were in here all night, and no one came to send us back to barracks?" Fitz asked. "Even after the zero-tolerance policy was instated?"

"That was eased after you brought Cadet Kung back," Hansen said. "But yes, we knew you five were here. And we knew what you were up to."

"Corrupting the files," Fitz said.

"Well, that was unexpected," Hansen said. "We knew you were working the case. There was no reason not to just let you run with it."

"You thought we'd figure it out for you?" Fitz asked.

"It seemed unlikely. But no reason not to let you try. It's a good learning experience, particularly if any of you choose the guardian track."

"We've solved a crime already, Ritchie and I," Fitz reminded him.

"Yes," Hansen allowed. "And you found Cadet Kung. That saved us hunting him down ourselves."

"Oh," Fitz said, wishing he could read something, anything, from Hansen's face. Because he couldn't tell: did command know about the sublevels of the academy? Did they know cadets went down there? Or did they think that Blaser had taken them to where Kung was hiding in one of the storage rooms at the end of that abandoned-looking hall-way? "What now, sir?"

"Now you can do what Keller and Wyss are already doing," Hansen said, getting up from his chair to lead Fitz to the door. "Go and take a brisk shower, then grab some chow. Your first class is at..." his eyes darted to one side as he consulted his implant. "0800. Your alert appearance and fully riveted attention are expected."

"Yes, sir," Fitz said.

"Do you know where Cadet Moreau and Cadet Ritchie are now?" Hansen asked as he opened the door to the library, now full with as bright a gray light as this miserable planet ever produced.

"They needed a moment alone, but they were going to meet me back here," Fitz said.

Hansen gave him a studied look, but then accepted his words at face value. "Then I shall wait for them here. Dismissed, cadet."

Fitz froze midstep out of the door and snapped back to attention to salute; then, after Hansen sketched a response to that gesture, he hurried away towards the barracks.

Did Hansen not know where Moreau and Ritchie were, or had that been a test?

And if it was a test, had Fitz passed?

21

"ARE YOU DOING OKAY?" Moreau asked Ritchie the moment that Fitz had left the hangar deck.

"Yeah," Ritchie said, but she knew she wasn't convincing. Especially with the way she had to squint her eyes against the harsh lighting. "I have a headache, but that's not a big deal. Nothing a nap and some decent food wouldn't take care of."

"Do you want to go get those?" Moreau asked.

"No, we should do this," Ritchie said.

"No, I meant, you get some sleep and food, and I'll check this out without you," Moreau said. "You can trust me, and I'll go get you the minute I know anything."

It was a very tempting offer. But in the end, Ritchie just shook her head. "No, I might as well see this through. I don't think I would have much of an appetite if presented with real food, and I definitely couldn't sleep."

"If you're sure?" Moreau said. Ritchie nodded. "The battery was through there, right?" she asked, pointing to the far side of the hangar deck.

"I've never been there either, but I believe so," Ritchie said.

They walked together across the deck and then into the smaller hallway. The lights kept winking on just ahead of where they were, but the lights here were more of a warm glow. The headache didn't go away, but it did quiet down a bit.

"This is it," Moreau said, putting her hand on the panel next to one of the doors.

"Are we allowed in there? I didn't even think of that," Ritchie said. "Neither of us has had the class yet. Maybe we're locked out."

"Nope," Moreau said when the panel under her hand switched from yellow to green. "We're good."

"It's open to all cadets, then," Ritchie said.

"It would've been a nuisance if it had locked us out," Moreau said.

"Yeah, but it would've slimmed down our list of suspects considerably."

The lights came on as they stepped inside the room, which was row after row of heavy-duty shelves with a narrow aisle running down the middle. The shelves closest to the doors were all empty but still had labels of what was meant to go where. As they went deeper in, they saw weapons lined up on the shelves, some reflecting the light from above with an oily sheen, but others covered with a fine layer of dust.

"No cleaning drones in this room, I guess," Moreau said. "Look, there's the inventory computer back there."

Ritchie let Moreau slide into the chair in front of the workstation and use her thumbprint to turn on the computer. She quickly clicked through screens. The first few looked like normal logs, cadets signing in and out various weapons.

"Why would someone sign out a weapon, do you think?" Ritchie asked as Moreau worked.

"Most of what's in this room are hand-held weapons, not vehicle-mounted weapons," Moreau said, running a fingertip down the screen to draw Ritchie's attention to the weapon types. "I'm guessing a lot of cadets want to gain extra proficiency scores before graduation. Especially ones who are intending to be guardians."

"What if someone didn't want to take a weapon out of this room? Like they wanted extra maintenance practice or something? Would that be on the log?" Ritchie asked.

"Yeah, look at this one," Moreau said. "That is a cannon meant to be mounted on a ground transport. This person, Cadet Falks, has his name in the user field, but there is no sign in or sign out information."

"Is this Cadet Falks our suspect, then?" Ritchie asked.

"Doubtful," Moreau said. "This record is from two years ago. It's 50/50, they've already graduated. Well, more likely, they graduated, since maintenance is an upper-level class." Then she turned in her chair to frown up at Ritchie. "There's nothing more recent."

"Maybe we're looking at the oldest files and not the newest," Ritchie suggested.

"No, look at the dates. Nothing is newer than nearly two years ago."

"But we know there've been classes since then, right? From this room? You guys found Egli's name on a list. Maybe we're in the wrong battery room," Ritchie said.

"No, this inventory is shared across all rooms," Moreau said. "Okay, I've been watching Wyss and Keller do this stuff for hours. Let's see..." her voice trailed off as she brought up a different window and started typing in commands that Ritchie didn't recognize. She tried something that did nothing and swore under her breath before trying again.

On the fourth try, she had brought up the logs. "Okay, this is you and me here," Moreau said. "And down here, that's all two years ago, just like on the other screens."

"But look at that one," Ritchie said, jabbing her finger at a line of text between the two groups. "Someone was in here already."

"It was a few hours ago," Moreau said with a frown. "And look there, that series of numbers? I think that means whoever touched the inventory system did it remotely."

"Not from this room?" Ritchie asked.

"Not from any of the battery rooms," Moreau said. "Maybe from somewhere else on campus?"

"We should get Wyss and Keller on this, shouldn't we?" Ritchie sighed, then reached her arms up in the air to stretch her back.

"Yeah," Moreau said, then sat up straighter in her chair. "The files aren't corrupted, though. I think they're still here."

"How can you tell?" Ritchie asked.

"It's like someone pulled the last two years of data and stuffed it in a file," Moreau said. "I think this one here. But it's encrypted."

"Encrypted, but not erased," Ritchie said hopefully.

"Depending on the level of encryption, this could be worse than erased," Moreau said, slumping back in her chair. Then she looked up at Ritchie again. "We're going to need Wyss and Keller. This is beyond me."

"Hey, everything you just did was pretty much beyond me," Ritchie said. "I'm feeling kind of superfluous."

"It's your investigation. I'm just helping," Moreau said.

They both fell silent for a moment. Neither was in a hurry to get up and go back out into that wind.

"Why is encryption worse than deletion?" Ritchie asked.

"Oh," Moreau said. "Wyss said that before, when he found out his files were corrupted. I guess he considered that a middle ground. Apparently, deleting things doesn't remove everything, and someone like Wyss can recreate the original data from what's left most of the time."

"But encrypted, you have to have the key to get into," Ritchie said.

"That, or a million years to try things," Moreau said. "Depending on how well it's encrypted."

"So if someone wanted to hide data, is encryption faster than deletion?" Ritchie asked.

"I don't know," Moreau said. "What are you thinking?"

"Well, we know whoever did all this is super smart, right?" Ritchie said. "They crashed Wyss's program and corrupted every file it was touching. How long would that take?"

"Wyss suspected whoever did it already had the program to do it ready to go. They would only need a second to insert it, preferably when he wasn't looking," Moreau said. "I gather he was in the bathroom at the time."

"I wonder if that was also done remotely?" Ritchie said. "Someone is watching us through the academy's own surveillance systems, aren't they?"

"That's creepy," Moreau said with a shiver.

"So our suspect takes down the program that's about to spit out their name, but they know these inventory computers weren't connected to the program at the time. So those files won't be corrupted," Ritchie said. "So they access them next. But they don't have time to go through all the steps of being sure they've deleted all traces, so they just encrypt what they don't want anyone to see and leave it."

"Leave it for what?" Moreau asked.

"Leave it until they do have enough time to delete all of it," Ritchie said. Then she threw up her hands. "It's all conjecture. I mean, it's been the middle of the night for most of this. Why wouldn't they be able to do it all without getting caught?"

"Because of Wyss, maybe?" Moreau said. "He's been going through so much information continuously all night long. I don't even know what half of his open windows are for."

"We should bring him out here," Ritchie said.

They both jumped as the door behind them beeped as it unlocked, then clanged as it swung open. But when they turned to look through the rows of shelves, they saw it was just Keller coming in.

"Hey," she called, giving them a little wave.

"Hey, Keller," Ritchie said. "What are you doing here?"

"Fitz told me where you were," she said. "He thought you might need some help."

"We were just talking about going to get Wyss," Moreau said. "We need to break into an encrypted folder."

"Let me see," Keller said, shooing Moreau out of the chair with little flicks of her hands. She leaned forward to peer at the screen. Then her hands started flying over the command panel. "Wyss is really busy, but I can handle this. It's pretty basic."

"You can decrypt it?" Ritchie asked, trying hard not to sound as skeptical as she felt. Keller was always the one poring over the communication aspects of her and Wyss's little projects. He had always been the programming guy.

"Oh, sure," Keller said, leaning back to dig through her pockets. She pulled something out of one of them and showed it to them before jamming it into the computer.

"What's that?" Ritchie asked.

"Decryption program," Keller said as she sat back and folded her arms as if awaiting her moment of triumph. "I usually let Wyss take the lead on the computer stuff because that's more his interest, but it's not because I lack any of the skills. It's just another language, and you know how I love learning languages."

"Yeah," Ritchie said. "I know."

"This program might take a while," Moreau said, putting a hand on Ritchie's arm. "Maybe now would be a good time for that nap."

"People were heading into breakfast when I was leaving," Keller said.

"Or a good time for food," Moreau said.

"No, I'm good," Ritchie said.

"You don't look good," Moreau said.

"Hey," Ritchie objected.

"Sorry, but it's true."

"If people are up and about, that means we're running out of time. The last thing I need is to be caught in the halls and thrown in detention for breaking curfew. I'm safer here."

"I think she's right," Keller said. "But if you just wanted a little food, the shuttles are stocked with ration packs. And there's always coffee in the command room."

"Isn't the command room locked?" Moreau asked.

Keller sat forward and ran her hands over the control panel, zipping through a series of screens before sitting back with an even bigger grin of triumph than before. "Not since I just unlocked it for you."

"Coffee does sound good," Ritchie said to Moreau's inquiring look.

"All right," Moreau said. "I'll see what I can find in the shuttles, and then I'll get some coffee and come right back."

"Thanks, Moreau," Ritchie said.

The door clanging shut behind Moreau sounded just a tad too final to Ritchie. Like she had just sealed Ritchie inside a tomb. With Keller.

"Ritchie?" Keller said, and Ritchie felt herself flinch. She had to remind herself that Keller was helping.

"Yeah?"

"You want the chair?" Keller asked, getting up without waiting for an answer and pushing Ritchie down into it. "You look beat."

"You've been up all night too," Ritchie said, but didn't have the strength to fight against the smaller cadet. She sank into the chair with an almost audible sigh of relief.

"I do it all the time, though. I've got a system," Keller said. Ritchie was afraid to ask just what she meant by that. She rubbed at the spot between her eyebrows where the headache had settled. "Food will help," Keller said, but not as if she believed it.

"Yeah," Ritchie said, not opening her eyes.

"I'm surprised you let Moreau do all the driving," Keller said. At Ritchie's questioning look, she added, "on the computer here."

"She's better at it," Ritchie said, closing her eyes once more.

"That's what I'm surprised about. It really is just another form of communication. And a really elegant one at that," Keller said. "And no matter what you insist, I know you have remarkable skills with languages. It comes up all the time in your dad's books."

The headache started to throb. Apparently, it liked Keller. It fed off Keller and her annoying, too eager voice.

"He always said he consulted with you," Keller went on, apparently not noticing Ritchie flinching in pain at each hot throb of that headache. "From the time you were a teeny tiny girl up until the day he was taken from us, he always asked you for your take on his work."

"I think whatever you've been reading was exaggerated," Ritchie said through gritted teeth. "It wasn't like that."

"Oh, tosh," Keller said. "I'm talking about his own books. The ones he wrote."

"Well, he didn't get a chance to write about that last mission," Ritchie said.

"No, not yet," Keller said.

Ritchie opened her eyes to look up at Keller, to see if she was telling a truly terrible joke or if she were serious. While Ritchie believed in her heart of hearts that her father still lived, the vast majority of the Union of Free Worlds were of the opinion that if the Yuffids hadn't killed him outright, they had certainly broken his mind.

But Keller wasn't standing over her anymore.

Ritchie turned in her chair to see if Keller was directly behind her, but the room around her was empty.

Then she heard a click from the door. But it wasn't followed by the clang of its opening.

"What did you do?" Ritchie asked as Keller came back down the aisle between the rows of weapons. "Did you lock that door? From the inside? What about Moreau?"

"Moreau can wait in the hallway, I think," Keller said as she all but skipped towards Ritchie, hands in her pockets. "I don't want her interrupting our little conversation."

Ritchie deeply regretted letting Moreau send Fitz back to the main building. She could really use him to be her Keller shield just at the moment.

She would just have to be her own shield. She had no choice. She had to be firm and shut Keller's questions down for good.

A part of her mind cried out that this wasn't the time. After a third night with no sleep, with that headache settled so low behind her eyes that it was darkening her vision, this wasn't the time to try to have this conversation. Her temper was on a very short fuse. She was going to say things she would regret later. So many things.

But the rest of her mind told that part to shut up. They had this under control.

"Listen, Keller," Ritchie said as reasonably as she could. "I understand why you're so interested in all this. And I know it should be super flattering. In all honesty, my father would've adored you. He would've wanted to mentor you if he could. But I'm not my father. I don't even have my father in my life anymore. Can you try to understand why talking about all this is painful for me?"

"No," Keller said, as chipper as ever. She was bouncing on her toes as she stood just out of arm's reach of Ritchie, as if she sensed the murderous rage about to boil over in Ritchie's mind.

Then she pulled her hands out of her pockets, and Ritchie realized the real reason why she was standing just out of reach.

So that Ritchie couldn't disarm her.

"I'm sorry it had to come to this," Keller said, holding the gun in one hand and bracing it with the other. Just like they'd been taught on the first day of small arms class. "You know how much I really, really like you. I'd hoped we'd become friends. But you've just been fighting me so much. Clearly, this is the only way to get you to open up."

"You don't have to do this," Ritchie said, slowly raising her hands in surrender.

"But I do!" Keller said. "Oh, don't worry. I don't want to kill you. I just need you to talk to me. You say it's painful for you to talk about all this. I'm just telling you, as of this moment now, it's going to be more painful if you don't."

She shifted her weight from foot to foot as if getting more comfortably into her firing stance. Then she rolled out her neck, never taking her eyes off of Ritchie sitting immobile in the chair.

Then she said, "now. Tell me about what happened on your father's last mission. Every detail. Start at the beginning."

22

FITZ WANTED nothing more than to get back to Ritchie and Moreau, to help them if they were still working on things or to know what they'd learned if they were not.

But the constant feeling of being watched was making his skin crawl. Some of the surveillance all the cadets knew about. The cleaning robots were always watchful, and everyone knew there were cameras at the ends of the barracks hallways to keep track of which cadets were in bunks and which were, with permission, working on something elsewhere on the school grounds.

But Hansen had known too much for that to be all he had access to.

"Hey," Stucki said as Fitz came into the room. "Didn't sleep last night?"

"Not really," Fitz said. Imhof and Stucki were both getting dressed, their hair still damp from the showers. The hall was full of cadets rushing to beat the others to the showers before breakfast, but Fitz was far too tired to try to hurry himself. He opened his locker but slumped down to sit on his bunk without grabbing anything out of it.

"What could you possibly be cramming for this soon in the semester?" Imhof asked with a dark frown.

"It wasn't classwork. It was a personal matter," Fitz said.

"Last night's curfew was strictly enforced. No one was supposed to be out of their bunks," Imhof said.

"I know," Fitz said, injecting a cheery tone to his voice just because he knew it would irritate Imhof. "I just came here now after meeting with Colonel Hansen. Everything is above board. But feel free to check up on me."

Imhof looked like he wanted to argue, but his eyes darted up and to the left, and Fitz knew he was checking the time. "You look a mess," he said instead. "And you're not smelling so great. Make sure to clean up before class."

"Yes, sir," Fitz said with a mocking salute. Imhof scowled but left the room without a word.

"He's actually trying to help you out, you know," Stucki said, checking his hair in the mirror one last time before slamming his locker closed.

"With unsolicited, yet overwhelmingly obvious, advice?" Fitz asked.

"Yeah, well," Stucki shrugged. But his face was still serious. "This is about your friend Cadet Ritchie; I take it?"

"Yeah," Fitz said.

"Did you find proof she's innocent?"

"We don't need to prove she's innocent," Fitz said. "There's no proof that she's guilty."

"You know what I meant," Stucki said, crossing his arms.

"No," Fitz said. For some reason, his throat had gotten tight. It was hard to get that one word out.

"You'll do it," Stucki said. "But Imhof wasn't wrong about your smell. Seriously, hit the showers."

Fitz nodded. Imhof's voice echoed down the hallway, calling Stucki's name.

"Gotta go," Stucki said. "See you in class."

The last of the cadets were coming out of the showers when Fitz was going in. He scrubbed himself clean as quickly as he could, then jogged back to his room. He tried to towel off and pull a clean uniform out of his locker at the same time, but he didn't have enough hands to pull it off.

He was just smoothing down his hair and rushing towards the door when he saw someone was lurking there, not quite in view.

It was Wyss. At first, it looked like Wyss was going to walk away, but then he changed his mind and turned to come back, colliding with Fitz, who was, by that time, standing in the doorway.

"Oh!" Wyss said, looking up at Fitz. "Sorry!"

"What's going on?" Fitz asked. "Are the others in trouble?"

"No," Wyss said, but he had dropped his eyes to look down at his own twisting hands. "Keller went to help Moreau and Ritchie with whatever they're working on."

"They aren't back yet?" Fitz asked. He had no doubt that if he bypassed the cafeteria, Hansen would know. There would be consequences. But if Ritchie needed his help...

"I wanted to talk to you," Wyss said, but Fitz barely heard him. He started to push past Wyss, to get upstairs and find Ritchie and Moreau. Wyss had to catch hold of Fitz's arm in both hands to pull him to a halt.

"What, Wyss?" Fitz asked, wrenching his arm free.

"I *need* to talk to you," Wyss said. His eyes were huge, imploring.

"Okay, I'm listening," Fitz said, turning the rest of the way around to face Wyss.

"It's about my program," Wyss said, hands twisting again. "About the malfunction."

"Okay," Fitz said again. It was all he could do not to scream at Wyss to just spit it out already. But clearly, Wyss was fighting some internal struggle. "You have a suspect?" he guessed.

Wyss nodded.

"But you're not sure," Fitz said. "You're afraid to say the name out loud in case you're wrong."

Wyss nodded again, looking even more miserable than before.

"Tell me," Fitz said, taking half a step closer. "We'll figure out together if you're right."

"It doesn't make any sense," Wyss said. "I'm sure I'm wrong. I shouldn't have said anything."

"Tell me," Fitz said.

Wyss continued to twist his hands, and Fitz forced himself to wait patiently. It was one of the hardest things he had ever done.

Finally, Wyss took a deep breath and started talking. "It was just Keller and me in the room, running the program. Moreau wasn't there at that point. We work alone together all the time, Keller and I, so that wasn't unusual."

"Sure," Fitz said. Was Wyss afraid that Fitz was going to accuse him of fraternizing with a fellow cadet?

"I had to step away," Wyss said.

"Step away?" Fitz asked, still picturing two cadets canoodling.

"To the bathroom," Wyss clarified. "I was only gone for a minute or two. But when I came back, the program had crashed. All of those files had been corrupted. And the list of names was gone."

"Wait a minute," Fitz said. "You're saying it was Keller?"

Wyss all but squirmed. "I don't want to. I don't want to believe it. But she was there."

"Could she do it?" Fitz asked. "Is that something she has the skill for, I mean?"

"She could totally do it," Wyss said. "She's learned a lot from me since we started working together last semester. She's a quick study."

"And she's good enough to where you couldn't find proof that it was her?" Fitz asked.

"Yesterday I would've said no," Wyss said. "Now, I'm not so sure."

"Right," Fitz said and spun on his heel to run up towards the main hall.

Wyss scrambled to catch up with him. "Wait, where are you going?"

"You said Keller went to help Moreau and Ritchie, right?" Fitz said. "If she tanked your program, she's not there to help."

"Oh, I guess not," Wyss said. "But she would never hurt Ritchie."

"From what we've seen, she's capable of quite a lot," Fitz said. They reached the main hallway, which was too crowded to keep running. Fitz pushed his way through cadets standing and chatting in groups as they lined up for breakfast. Wyss got hung up briefly, but then burst out of the throng to catch up with Fitz at the entrance to the library.

"What do you mean?" Wyss asked. "All she did was crash my program."

"Are you kidding me?" Fitz asked. "She's obviously the murderer."

"Whoa! I never said that!" Wyss objected.

"Why else would she kill your program and corrupt all those files?" Fitz asked.

"Because of Ritchie," Wyss said.

Fitz stopped abruptly at the first of the library's doors to the outside. "What's that supposed to mean?" he asked.

"I just assumed she did it to protect Ritchie," Wyss said. "The program must have implicated her. That would absolutely crush Keller. Ritchie is like a hero to her. She'd do anything to protect her."

"I don't buy it," Fitz said. "We were all there to protect Ritchie. If that was what Keller was trying to do, she had no reason to be under-handed about it."

"Really? If we had found actual proof of Ritchie's guilt, we would've all agreed together to destroy it? Really?" Wyss asked.

Fitz scowled. "Maybe not you. But Ritchie didn't do it."

"Do we know that for a fact?" Wyss asked.

"I know it in my bones," Fitz said. Wyss rolled his eyes. "No, listen to me. I would do anything for Ritchie. I owe her more than I could ever repay. And Ritchie trusts me, too. We both know that Keller has been more than a little obsessed with Ritchie since she and I got here. Is there any universe where Keller doesn't know about that bond between Ritchie and I? Think about it."

"She knows," Wyss said. "She's mentioned it on a few occasions. She thinks you're beneath Ritchie."

"Well, who doesn't?" Fitz said. "But never mind that. Keller also trusts you, doesn't she?"

"I thought she did until last night," Wyss said.

"So if it's true what you conjectured, that Keller deleted proof of Ritchie's guilt, why would she wait for you to step away to do it? Why didn't she just ask you to trust her? Why didn't she tell me to do it? I'm all about taking the blame."

"I don't know," Wyss said. "I still think she was trying to protect Ritchie. But maybe she wanted to be a hero?"

"Now that makes sense," Fitz said. "That sounds like Keller."

"So, what do we do now?" Wyss asked.

Fitz looked out into the gray morning. Although there was still no sign of the sun, at least the wind had died down.

"I'm going to go find them," he said. "I want to hear what Keller has to say for herself. But maybe you should head back to breakfast. I have a feeling skipping classes is about to have consequences."

"No," Wyss said. "You can be there, but I have to be the one who confronts Keller."

Fitz met Wyss's eyes and saw the younger cadet was deadly serious. There was some anger in him, directed at Keller and her maybe betrayal of their friendship. But there was also a distrust of Fitz.

"Fine, then," Fitz said. "But keep up."

Then he pushed his way outside and ran down the gravel path towards the underground hangar.

23

RITCHIE KEPT her hands up in the air and her eyes on Keller. She sat very still and kept her breath slow and even.

But her mind was running at full speed, cataloging everything she remembered about the room around her, ranking every potential weapon. How much hurt could she inflict with it? How quickly could she get her hands on it?

Not that she wanted to hurt Keller. But she didn't want to risk getting shot, either. And she kept having flashes of memory of her fight with Weld in the train car on her way to the academy. She had had to fight for her life that day, and she knew she had done it well. But that hadn't stopped the nightmares of being thrown out into the wind by a crazed cadet to fall to her death on the rocky mountainside far, far below.

Whatever happened next, no matter how well she handled it, she was going to be living with those consequences, too.

And that was on top of the nightmares that still plagued about the day her father was taken away. Was this what her life was always going to be? Just layer after layer of trauma until finally her mind just broke down?

"I told you to start talking," Keller said, gesturing with the gun like she wanted to poke Ritchie with it. Alas, she didn't step any closer forward. She was too far out of reach for Ritchie to try tackling her.

"I thought we were friends," Ritchie said.

"We are friends," Keller said. "Best friends."

"And yet you never seem to notice what a painful topic this is for me," Ritchie said. "Friends have empathy."

"Don't lecture me about friendship," Keller said. "I'm way better at it than you are."

"Really?" Ritchie said, then flinched as she heard the disdain in her own voice. She had been caught off guard by that remark, but she really shouldn't be provoking Keller just now.

"Of course I am," Keller said, flapping her elbows as if she wanted to both throw up her hands in exasperation but at the same time not stop aiming the gun. "You and I are friends, but that friendship is all on me. I do all the work. But that's okay! Despite what you think, I know what happened to your father hurt you. I take that into account every time I talk to you. I know it means I have to be twice the friend to bridge that gap, but I'm happy to do it."

"What do you mean?" Ritchie asked, genuinely confused.

"You're frequently rude," Keller said. "But I let that go. I don't take it personally. Because I'm the bigger person."

"If I'm so rude, why do you still want to be friends?" Ritchie asked.

"Because I know it's just because of all these things you're going through."

"What things?" Ritchie asked. What happened to her father, even in Keller's mind, could only count as one thing. So what else was she talking about?

"You were super nice when you got here," Keller said. "Don't you remember the first day we met? And we talked—actually talked—about alien communication systems, and it was absolutely lovely."

"I remember," Ritchie said. And she did. They *had* had a nice conversation that day. A nice general conversation that was relevant to something that came up in one of Keller's classes. A conversation that had never touched on Ritchie's father, not even once.

"But then Jeger happened," Keller said, narrowing her eyes. "She lit into you on your second day here, and she just never let up again."

Ritchie thought of how her trouble with Jeger actually began the minute Ritchie had stepped off the train platform, before she had even set eyes on the school itself. But she didn't say so. Keller didn't seem like she was open to data that didn't already fit her theory.

"Everything here got hard and didn't let up," Ritchie said instead. "I was overwhelmed. I'm sorry if any of that blew back on you."

"Like I said, I knew why you were... terse," Keller said, nodding to herself over that word choice. "I let it go."

"And now?" Ritchie asked, gesturing with her hands that were still raised in surrender. "What changed now?"

"What do you mean what changed?" Keller demanded. "Everything changed! Everything but you, that is. Jeger is gone, out of your life forever. But you still won't talk to me."

"Not about my father, I won't," Ritchie said. "It's not about you. I don't dredge up that past for anyone. A friend wouldn't keep pushing me to."

"You've never had a better friend than me," Keller said. "After everything I did for you."

"What did you do?" Ritchie asked.

"You must know," Keller said. "You must've figured it out."

She glanced past Ritchie to the computer screen, and Ritchie turned her head to see what she was looking at.

"I thought your program was going to decrypt that folder," Ritchie said.

"I deleted it," Keller said. "Just like I deleted all the others. It's not fast, but my program gets it done. All the evidence is gone now. Not even Wyss could retrieve it. We're all safe."

"Who's 'we?'" Ritchie asked. Her ears were starting to ring, and the room felt unsteady around her. Like the whole world was chaos, and she was helplessly lost in it. Like the first time she had flown her glider, before she had learned to feel the wind. "What did you do, Keller?"

"I saved you," she said.

"By deleting the surveillance feeds and the logs?" Ritchie asked. She swallowed down the bitter taste building at the back of her throat. "Because I know I wasn't on them, Keller. I couldn't have been."

"No, you weren't," Keller said, "but I was."

"Please," Ritchie said, wracking her brain for Keller's first name. She needed the younger cadet to feel like they were connected on a personal level. But what was it? She had heard it once. Then she had it. "Sidonie, what did you do?"

"You know what I did," Keller said. "I gave you a gift. Such a gift!"

"Sidonie, did you kill Jeger?" Ritchie asked. "Please, please say that you didn't."

"I did more than kill her!" Keller said. "I rigged it so that *you* could kill Jeger. I gave you that."

"I didn't want that!" Ritchie said.

"You needed to do it. Now you have closure."

Ritchie put her pounding head in her hands, wishing she could shut out Keller's voice. But she couldn't. And her mind couldn't stop going over every minute she had ever spent with Keller, everything Ritchie had said, and everything Ritchie had done. Was there something there that had made Keller believe that killing Jeger was what she wanted?

"Someone else could've gotten hurt," Ritchie said. "If I had shot at Fitz—"

"You wouldn't've," Keller said firmly. "Every combat situation I ever watched you fly, you never took a shot at Fitz. And you had some nice opportunities. Jeger even chewed you out for it one time, don't you remember?"

Ritchie didn't try to. She didn't want to think of Jeger at all. She was afraid if she did, she'd break down for sure.

"What if I had shot someone else?" she asked instead.

"Didn't you hear me? You couldn't have," Keller said. Ritchie's face was still in her hands, but she sensed Keller moving closer, leaning in as if to be sure Ritchie could hear her. But not close enough for Ritchie to get the gun from her. "Why did you think I was helping Wyss with that drone swarm project? You didn't really think I was interested in improving tactical modeling, did you?"

"You know, I did," Ritchie said, lifting her face to look at Keller. The younger cadet still had her gun trained on Ritchie. "I thought you and

Wyss were a team, working together to advance both of your knowledge."

"The language stuff, sure," Keller said. "But the drones I just needed so I could see what was going on up there. You know, I really thought it was going to take most of the semester for you to get it done. I expected that Wyss and I would have to really dazzle command so we could keep observing the combat flight drills, even though we were supposed to be in class at the time. But you were amazing! First opportunity, you nailed it."

"You used me," Ritchie said. "You murdered someone by using me as a weapon. Without my consent."

"But that's the beauty of it," Keller said. "I did it for you. Someday you'll thank me. I can wait."

Ritchie wrapped her arms around her stomach as if she could hug the sour ache away. Keller was clearly crazy, but had Ritchie somehow lead her towards this murderous path? Did she bear some part of the blame?

They both jumped at the sudden echoing sound of a click at the door. Someone being denied entry by the locking system.

"I guess Moreau's back," Keller said, taking a few steps backward down the aisle, but the gun on Ritchie never wavering. "I actually expected her back sooner. Shame she can't get in."

Ritchie heard Moreau's voice, but only dimly through the thick metal door. She spoke, then knocked, then spoke again.

"She won't give up," Ritchie said.

Keller scoffed. "Like it matters. She can't get past my locking mechanism. Not even Wyss could do it."

"She's going to go for help," Ritchie said to Keller. Keller frowned as if she hadn't considered that possibility.

"Yeah, I guess you're right," Keller said. "Well, there's nothing else to be done. I guess it's two hostages."

"Maybe you should tie me up first?" Ritchie said.

"Look, you can't outsmart me, so don't even try," Keller said. "I know you don't want to help me."

"I don't want Moreau in here," Ritchie said. "I don't want to risk you hurting her. I'll do whatever it takes to keep her safe."

"Noble," Keller scoffed. "But in this moment you can't do anything, let alone 'whatever it takes.' You can just keep sitting in that chair while I deal with this."

Ritchie looked past Keller, towards the door. She widened her eyes and let a momentary flush of happiness wash over her, then steeled her expression again.

Keller narrowed her eyes suspiciously, but Ritchie just put her hands back in the surrender position and said nothing.

Then Keller turned her head to look towards the door, to see whatever Ritchie must have seen that had filled her with such happiness and relief.

But there was nothing there, just the locked door and the soft pounding from Moreau on the other side.

She turned back to Ritchie. Perhaps she was about to say something about how it was impossible to fool her, how she still had the upper hand. But Ritchie didn't particularly want to hear it. In the brief few seconds when Moreau's head had been turned, she had gotten to her feet and stepped aside.

Now she flung the chair down the aisle straight at Moreau, ducking just as the gun went off.

24

DESPITE HAVING BEEN RUNNING since he left the library, when Fitz reached the hallway on the far side of the hangar deck and heard the sound of someone pounding on a door, he found an extra reserve of energy to sprint.

It was Moreau pounding on a door and yelling Keller and Ritchie's names. She heard his feet pounding down the hall and stepped back from the door, pushing loose hair out of her eyes.

"It's Keller!" she told him as he slapped his own hand on the locking mechanism. "She's in there with Ritchie. She did something to the door. I knew she had a weird vibe, but I told myself I was just going crazy from sleep deprivation."

"Can you hear them in there?" Fitz asked, pressing his ear to the door. He could hear something like the sound of a struggle, but it was so muffled he wasn't sure.

"Step back," Wyss said as he finally caught up. He was red-faced and winded, but didn't stop to catch his breath. The minute Fitz and Moreau had stepped back, he took a tool out of his pocket and pried open the front of the locking mechanism.

"It worked before," Moreau said. "I don't know what she did."

"I have an idea," Wyss said grimly.

"Can you get in from here?" Fitz asked.

"She's got a scrambler on the other side of this panel," Wyss said. "I can get past it, but it's going to take a minute."

Fitz turned to Moreau. "Go get Colonel Hansen."

Moreau gave him a quick nod, then took off down the hallway at top speed.

"How can I help?" Fitz asked. Panic was threatening to overwhelm him. Yet another locked door between him and Ritchie when she was in danger. It was maddening.

When this was over, he was going to make sure Wyss taught him how to defeat door security.

Wyss was still poking around inside the panel. He neither looked up nor slowed in his work as he said, "get to the control room. There are portable computers in there, the kinds used to run diagnostics in the shuttles. Bring me one of those."

"Got it," Fitz said. But he had only taken four or five steps, not yet even at a running pace, when he heard a loud clang. He skidded to a halt and spun around.

Wyss was standing up and backing away from the panel and now-open doorway. His eyes were wide, but Fitz couldn't see what he was reacting to.

"Ritchie!" Fitz yelled and dashed back to the doorway.

Ritchie was on the inside, some sort of electronic disk in one hand, a gun in the other. Her hair was in complete disarray, and there was a long scratch down her cheek.

"Hey," Ritchie said to both of them, then thrust the disk at Wyss. He took it, then stepped back to examine it. "Maybe save that for later. The dongle she stuck in that computer is the more important thing."

"Where is she?" Fitz asked, trying to look around Ritchie into the room beyond.

"Over by the computer," Ritchie said. "I hit her with a chair. A couple of times."

"Are you okay?" Fitz asked.

Ritchie looked surprised. "Fine. I mean, a nap would be great, but other than that."

"She didn't hurt you?"

Ritchie gave a humorless laugh. "Have you seen Keller in hand to hand drills? It wasn't much of a fight."

Fitz frowned. This sort of bravado wasn't like Ritchie at all. It felt like a defense mechanism. Like she was putting up a wall between them. He didn't like it at all. If Wyss hadn't been there with them, he might have called her out on it.

But Wyss was there.

"I'm guessing she had that gun, though," Fitz said instead.

"She did," Ritchie said. "Come on. I need Wyss to look at that computer. You can help me make sure that Keller is secured."

"She came here to erase evidence, didn't she?" Wyss asked as Ritchie led the way down the narrow aisle between shelves of weapons.

"Yes, but even before that, it wasn't accessible to Moreau and me, and maybe not even to command," Ritchie said. "She encrypted it. She said she was running a decryption program, but I think all she did was unlock it herself and then start deleting all traces of evidence against her."

Then they reached the spot where Ritchie had left Keller sprawled out on the floor. The chair was in several pieces scattered among the shelves and around the computer workstation.

"You knocked her out?" Fitz asked as Wyss raced to the computer and started tapping away at it.

"I had to," Ritchie said. "I hit her with the chair, but she still had the gun. You can see where she shot at me but hit that wall back there."

"Ritchie, I see three burn marks," Fitz said.

"She wouldn't let go of the gun," Ritchie said. "I had to keep hitting her with the chair."

Fitz knew a heavily edited version of events when he heard one. But he could also see that Ritchie was struggling to keep her composure. And not entirely succeeding: she pushed her hair back from her eyes with the hand that still held the gun, a breach of safety protocol she would never do in normal circumstances.

Then he saw the gap in the shoulder of her uniform, a burn mark where laser fire had blasted through. He pulled Ritchie closer to make sure her arm underneath was unharmed.

"Oh," Ritchie said, surprised.

"You don't feel that?" Fitz asked, looking at the blistered welt that crossed her shoulder.

"I do now, actually," she said. It was like Fitz could watch the blood drain out of her face.

"Sit down," he commanded, taking the gun from her and helping her to sit down on the floor. "Is there anything in here to tie Keller up with?"

"Her own clothes?" Ritchie suggested. Her eyes were closed, and she had rolled her head back to rest on the shelf behind her.

Fitz started to look around for anything better, but then saw that Keller was starting to stir. He kicked the larger pieces of chair out of her reach and trained the gun on her as her eyelids fluttered, then opened.

Her pupils were different sizes, and she couldn't seem to get him into focus, but even so, she was grinning up at him.

"Hey, Fitz," she slurred. "Did Ritchie tell you what I did?"

"Try not to talk," he said, pushing her back down with his foot when she tried to sit up. "And stay where you are. Command is on their way."

"It's not a clean deletion," Wyss said. "There's enough left for me to work with."

"What is it, can you tell?" Fitz asked.

"Not yet," Wyss said. "I can patch it back together, but it's going to take some time."

"She did it," Ritchie said weakly. She rolled her head to one side as she opened her eyes to look at Fitz.

"All of it?" Fitz asked, never taking his eyes off of Keller. "We knew she was removing the evidence, but Wyss and I disagreed about what that meant."

"I think we're in agreement now," Wyss said dryly. "If Ritchie had to hit her with a chair, that means you were right."

"You knew?" Ritchie asked.

"We were just figuring it out," Fitz said. "I got here as fast as I could. I'm so sorry, Ritchie." He wanted more than anything to look over at her, to be sure she knew how much he meant that, but he didn't dare look away from Keller even for a moment. He could see the way she was moving her feet and hands. At the slightest of opportunities, she would spring back to her feet. Who knew what she'd do then.

"You probably knew before I did, then," Ritchie said with a laugh that threatened to break down into sobs. "Even when she pulled that gun on me, I still thought she just wanted to talk about my dad."

"I did just want to talk about your dad," Keller said. "I have to know what happened when he met the Yuffids. What went wrong?"

Fitz felt his blood run cold. How he wished he had something to gag Keller with.

"She killed Jeger," Ritchie said. "She set up the gun and used Wyss's drones to figure out the timing. Then she deleted all the evidence that she had ever done anything at all."

"Starting with the trigger signal," Wyss said, straightening up and turning away from the computer as that thought sank into his mind. "You've been working against me the entire time?"

"And you never knew, did you?" Keller asked with a sly grin.

Wyss's pale skin grew even paler. "I trusted you," he said. "We've been working together nearly every day since we met. And this whole time, you were a monster?"

"I'm not a monster," Keller said.

"But I don't understand," Wyss said, his eyes darting from Fitz to Ritchie and back again. "Why did she kill Jeger? We never even had any classes with her. Not as novice cadets. Jeger never did anything to her. It makes no sense."

"It was a gift," Ritchie said. "A gift for me."

Fitz felt like he was going to be sick. He could only imagine how Ritchie felt.

"But why?" Wyss asked.

"Because I need her to tell me what happened in that meeting between her father and the Yuffids," Keller said. "Jeger was a distraction that had to be eliminated. Now Ritchie is free to focus on other things. She'll tell me everything she knows about what happened. And then I'll finally have what I need to unlock that mystery. It will make my career!"

"Your career?" Fitz said, incredulous. "Don't you realize what you've done? What happens next? You're not going to have a career now. You're going to be locked away for the rest of your life."

"I'm sure that's true," Keller said. "But it won't matter. I have skills the Union of Free Worlds are going to need. And no matter where I am, locked away or not, they'll come to me because they won't have any choice. I don't need to wear a diplomat's uniform to do what I do best."

"She's crazy," Wyss said, shaking his head sadly.

"That doesn't mean I'm not right," Keller said, raising her chin defiantly.

"Well, here's the thing," Fitz said. "Your plan seems to rely on you unlocking the secrets of the Yuffid. Which you can't do without Ritchie's help. And she's never going to help you."

"I can crack it without her," Keller said, but for the first time, there was a hint of uncertainty in her tone.

"You never should've tried to mess with her," Fitz said. "That was your fatal mistake."

There was the sound of voices approaching down the hallway, and Keller, Ritchie, and Wyss all looked towards the door. But Fitz remained as he was, eyes and gun both focused unwaveringly on Keller until the guards had her on her belly on the floor and her hands behind her back in restraints.

"Cadets," Colonel Hansen said with little nods to Ritchie, Wyss, and then Fitz. He raised an eyebrow. "Cadet Fitz, where did you get that gun?"

"Keller had it," Ritchie said. "I took it from her. I have no idea where she got it from."

"I'll take it now," Hansen said, and Fitz handed it over.

"Where's Moreau?" Fitz asked. All he saw were security forces. And not anyone actually stationed on Oymyakon. This squad was from somewhere else, somewhere more official.

"I sent her on to class," Hansen said. "Which is where the three of you are going."

"I'm still running—" Wyss started to say, gesturing to the computer behind him.

"We'll take it from here," one of the new guards told him.

"But—" Wyss tried to object.

"There will be a debriefing for each of you after classes," Hansen said.

"Sir, Ritchie was injured," Fitz said, pointing to her shoulder.

"It's nothing," Ritchie said, but couldn't hide the wince as the colonel pulled the fabric of her tunic aside to examine the wound.

"I guess that's one more missed class for you, cadet," Hansen sighed. "Infirmary. Now. Unless you need transport there?"

"I can walk," Ritchie said, getting to her feet.

"Stay with her," Hansen said to Fitz and Wyss.

"Yes, sir," they said together.

Fitz waited until they were in the cavernous space of the hangar deck before saying, "Hansen told me a team of experts we're on their way. I guess that was them."

"The corrupted files?" Ritchie asked.

"They have copies," Fitz said. "Probably the ones Keller came down here to delete as well. She's not as clever as she thinks she is."

"Yeah, she is," Wyss said. "She's just not the cleverest."

The three of them climbed up the ramp to the edge of the open field. Still no sun, but the wind was a mere hair-tousling breeze, and the clouds were high above, crossing the sky at a lazy pace.

"Can I ask a delicate question?" Wyss asked.

"Is it about the Yuffids?" Fitz asked before Ritchie could respond.

"Yeah," Wyss admitted.

"Then no," Fitz said. "Absolutely not."

"Fair enough," Wyss said.

They walked the rest of the way to the infirmary in silence.

25

IT WAS ALWAYS uncomfortable being in the colonel's office, but it was twice as uncomfortable to be there when he wasn't.

Ritchie sat primly in the chair across from his, and resisted the urge to touch the things on his desktop. She wished he had left something displayed there, his day planner or notes, or anything that would give her a hint as to why he had pulled her out of class. And just her, not Moreau or even Fitz.

She jumped to her feet as the door opened and the colonel came in.

"Cadet Ritchie," he said. "At ease." She sank back down onto the chair, carefully smoothing down the back of her uniform as she sat. "I suppose you're wondering why I called you here."

"Yes, sir," she said. "I thought the investigation was closed?"

"Yes, that's all over," he said as he sat down behind his desk.

"May I ask when the trial begins?" she asked.

"There won't be a trial," Hansen said. "Sidonie Keller confessed to everything."

"I guess I'm not surprised to hear that, sir," Ritchie said. "What happens to her now?"

"Much the same as happened with Cadmar Weld," he said. "She's been committed to the same station, in fact."

"What does that mean?" Ritchie asked.

"It means that like Weld, she will never be in a position to hurt anyone ever again," Hansen said. "She'll be treated by experts in the field, but after her initial evaluation, it seems very unlikely she'll ever be released."

"She seemed to think that she'll still be working for the Union of Free Worlds," Ritchie said.

"How's that?" Hansen asked.

"I don't know what she was thinking, but she said that wherever she ended up, her skills would prove too valuable for the Union to pass up," Ritchie said. Then, hesitantly, she asked, "Is she right, sir?"

Hansen rubbed at a barely visible smudge on the edge of his desk for a long moment, not looking up at her. "She might be. Yes, I think that is a possibility. If the Union ever sees a use for her, she will be put to it. But not released. She'll never be out in public again."

Ritchie shuddered, especially at the word "use." It sounded so clinical.

"Is it a coincidence she's in the same place as Weld?" she asked.

Hansen glanced up at her. "You ask all the important questions, don't you?"

"Sir?"

"To be honest, cadet, I don't know. It is the largest observational facility station in this quadrant. It could be just a coincidence. Or it could be a part of something I'm not privy to. Above my pay grade, as it were."

"Yes, sir," Ritchie said, although she didn't really understand.

"I called you in here because Sidonie Keller made a request," he said. "She wanted to maintain a correspondence with you. I am required to inform you of this, but you are not required to agree to it."

"Correspondence, like video calls?" Ritchie asked.

"No, it would all be in writing," he said. "And every message you receive or send will be reviewed by the team supervising her care before it is passed on."

"What's the point of it, sir?" Ritchie asked.

"To whom?" Hansen asked, but went on before Ritchie could answer. "For the staff at the observational facility, I'm sure it's considered therapeutic. For Keller, another chance to grill you about your father." Surprise must have registered on her face because Hansen gave her a little nod. "Yes, I know about her fascination with your father's work."

"So even now, she wants to keep asking me about the Yuffids?" Ritchie asked.

"I'm sure she does," Hansen said. "Which is why I would suggest that you ignore this request. You have enough to focus on here with your studies. You don't need the added distraction. But it's not my place to make that decision; it's yours. The only other thing I'd say is that if you are thinking of agreeing to this proposition, be very clear in your mind what you want to get out of it. You'll need to have the parameters well defined before embarking on that mission."

"You think I'm going to say yes?" Ritchie asked.

"Aren't you?"

"But you just told me not to," she said.

"It was my strong suggestion," he said. "The decision is yours."

Ritchie looked down at her hands folded in her lap. Hansen waited patiently as she thought it all through.

"I think I'd like to say yes," she said at last. Hansen was clearly disappointed, but he just nodded. "I'd like an opportunity to help her therapeutically," she said.

"The facility staff certainly holds that hope as well," he said.

"You don't think it will help?" Ritchie guessed.

"It doesn't matter what I think," he said. "She's no longer a cadet at this academy, but you are. My strongest concern is naturally going to be you and your readiness for a career in foreign service."

"Yes, sir," Ritchie said.

"Take a few days to think it over before giving me your final answer," he said.

"Yes, sir," Ritchie said, getting up from her chair. She saluted and left the office, then headed towards the cafeteria. She had missed the end of class and could hear the cadets gathering for lunch. She slowed her steps, then stopped entirely, ducking into an alcove and leaning against the wall. She wasn't ready to be around other people just yet.

She wanted to care about Keller's therapy. But the truth was, she didn't. She could hardly be surprised that Keller clung to any thread of connection between them, no matter how tenuous.

And Ritchie could cut it off so easily. She just had to say no.

But if she said no, she lost any chance of someday understanding why Keller had done what she did. If Ritchie had done something that had led Keller to believe killing Jeger was, as she said, a gift.

It might take years for Keller to get to a place where she could understand and speak about her own motivations. She might not ever get there.

But if there was any chance at all of getting an answer, Ritchie had to take it. She had to know. Because this had happened twice now. She needed to know if she was doing something she could change, or if she was just cursed.

THE OYMYAKON FOREIGN Service Academy had a memorial service for Cadet Hanne Jeger. Cadet Lieutenant Nicol Egli was promoted to cadet captain. And after about a week, no one really seemed to even remember that anything had happened.

Not that Fitz didn't understand the forgetting. Not with the coursework that started piling on exponentially during that week. And he had more of it than anyone since he had extra work details as part of his academic probation.

But he didn't like it, that feeling like life just went back to normal in such a hurry. To him, nothing was the same. But he had no one to share his feelings with.

Finally, it was the weekend. A weekend full of homework and kitchen duty, but a weekend all the same. After he finished cleaning up from breakfast and was dismissed, he ran immediately to the library, the one place he was always sure to find Ritchie.

He walked past all the reading nooks and up and down the long study table, but there was no sign of her.

But the last in the row of meeting rooms had its walls set to opaque.

He told himself there was no way she was in there. Why would any of them be in there? Even Wyss must have found a different place to do his thing, now that this place was tainted by the memory of his former partner.

But when he knocked, he could scarcely call himself surprised when Moreau opened the door.

"Oh, hey," she said, stepping aside to let him in. "I told you he'd be here," she said as she walked back to the table.

"What are we doing?" Fitz asked as he closed the door, then joined Moreau with Ritchie and Wyss at the table.

"Well, the first item on the agenda is talking Ritchie out of being Keller's pen pal," Moreau said.

"What?" Fitz asked.

"It's not up for debate," Ritchie said. She had gotten her hair cut since the last time he'd seen her. Something very short that stood up, then fell in a gentle wave over the top of her head. "I need to keep tabs on her."

"Why?" Fitz asked.

Ritchie chewed at her lip for a moment as Moreau and Fitz both waited for her answer. For his part, Wyss seemed involved in whatever he was doing on the screen in front of him. As usual.

"I just do," she said at last.

"That's a terrible answer," Moreau said. Then she turned to Fitz. "Did you know Keller is in the same facility as Weld?"

"She is?" Fitz asked.

"What if they form a little Murdina Ritchie fan club?" Moreau asked. "They're both crazy."

"But in different ways," Ritchie said.

"And they're both smart," Moreau went on as if she hadn't been interrupted.

"And under constant observation," Ritchie said.

"Would you tell her this is a bad idea?" Moreau pleaded to Fitz.

Fitz looked at Ritchie. "No," he said. "If Ritchie has her reasons, that's good enough for me. I mean, it would be nice if she *shared* them."

"Wouldn't it?" Moreau said wistfully.

"Aren't you worried she's just going to keep grilling you about your dad?" Wyss asked.

"I don't have to answer anything I don't want to," Ritchie said. "She can ask all she likes."

"You're still letting her into your head," Moreau said.

"Maybe," Ritchie said, but she didn't sound worried at the possibility.

"Ritchie can handle it," Fitz said.

"Well, this was lovely, but I really have a ton of studying to do," Ritchie said, getting up from the table. Moreau stood up as well. "Until next week?"

"Same time, same place," Wyss said, giving her a little wave. Ritchie headed out the door, but Fitz caught Moreau before she could follow.

"How is she really?"

"Better," Moreau said. "Especially after the announcement about Keller being guilty, and that Ritchie was absolutely not an accomplice. That could've come a lot sooner, but better late than never."

"Let me know if anyone is still hassling her," Fitz said.

Moreau scowled at him. "She's my buddy. I've got this."

"Of course you do," Fitz said, but she was already gone.

"You know Ritchie from before, don't you?" Wyss said, looking up from his screen for the barest of moments.

"Yeah," Fitz said, settling back into his chair. He had a ton of homework himself, and another shift of kitchen duty in the morning, but he was in no hurry to get to it.

"Do you know what happened with her father? You know, with the Yuffids?" Wyss asked.

"Why are you bringing that up? I told you before, there'd be no answers to those questions," Fitz said.

"Oh, sorry," Wyss said. "I thought it was just Ritchie that I wasn't supposed to ask. I didn't realize it was personal to you, too."

"Well, it is," Fitz said. "It happened years ago. Why is everyone so obsessed with it? The Yuffids left, and they're never coming back."

"They haven't yet," Wyss said. "Doesn't mean they never will."

Fitz frowned. Hadn't Jeger said something about the Yuffids as well? That last morning before she died?

"I should go," Fitz said. Wyss nodded without looking up, and Fitz let himself out of the room and then out of the library.

He headed down to the barracks, fully intending to get every assignment done to absolute perfection. As much as he hated course work and would rather be doing something else. Because if he got expelled, he would lose more than his future career in the foreign service. He would lose the ability to stay close to Ritchie.

Because this Yuffid stuff was clearly going to keep coming up. And he had to be there with her to be her shield.

He owed it to her. And he refused to let her down.

CHECK OUT BOOK THREE

The Ritchie and Fitz Sci-Fi Murder Mysteries will continue with Book Three, Body in the Catacombs.

Murdina Ritchie and Shackleton Fitz IV start their junior year at the Oymyakon Foreign Service Academy finally feeling like they belong in that world. They stand as equals among the other cadets. And the crushing load of schoolwork? Surprisingly manageable when you're not trying to solve a murder at the same time.

But the rumors of big changes in the political universe reach even the depths of the Academy. Distrust and secretiveness invade the minds of all of the cadets. Something dark and tumultuous hangs over all of them, and not just the ever-present storms of Oymyakon.

Then someone finds a body in the lower levels, and the accusations fly. A murder, but committed decades before. Long before the time of any of the cadets.

But not before the time of the instructors. In fact, exactly at the time Colonel Hansen was Cadet Hansen.

Can Ritchie and Fitz solve the coldest of cases and prove the colonel innocent? Or worse, guilty?

Body in the Catacombs, book three in the Ritchie and Fitz Sci-Fi Murder Mystery series.

NEW SERIES: THE FORGOTTEN PLANET

Coming soon from Ratatoskr Press Books, the new YA sci-fi series *The Forgotten Planet* starts with book 1: *Raiding the Forgotten Derelict*.

History sleeps beneath them all, but only she sees it.

Lafayette Eloi always knew her parents thought differently from others. They kept their books buried beneath her mother's house. They spoke an old language in the dead of night, whispering behind closed doors and bolted shutters. She grew up in a village where no one was related to her, and she never knew why.

Then, after her mother died, her father came to fetch her. Now she and her mother's dog assist her father in his work. The work discussed in whispers in the dark. The work that had cost Lafayette so much all her young life.

But now she learns just how much her father's work means to their entire world. Only no one knows anything about it. Only her father. And only Lafayette.

Because the work that consumed her father's entire life and her mother's too now nibbles at the fringe's of Lafayette's own life. And she cannot refuse its call.

Raiding the Forgotten Derelict, first book in the new YA sci-fu series *The Forgotten Planet,* available in September 2024 from Ratatoskr Press Books.

COMPLETE SERIES: THE RITCHIE AND FITZ SCI-FI MURDER MYSTERIES

The Ritchie and Fitz Sci-Fi Murder Mysteries starts with *Murder on the Intergalactic Railway.*

For Murdina Ritchie, acceptance at the Oymyakon Foreign Service Academy means one last chance at her dream of becoming a diplomat for the Union of Free Worlds. For Shackleton Fitz IV, it represents his last chance not to fail out of military service entirely.

Strange that fate should throw them together now, among the last group of students admitted after the start of the semester. They had once shared the strongest of friendships. But that all ended a long time ago.

But when an insufferable but politically important woman turns up murdered, the two agree to put their differences aside and work together to solve the case.

Because the murderer might strike again. But more importantly, solving a murder would just have to impress the dour colonel who clearly thinks neither of them belong at his academy.

Murder on the Intergalactic Railway, the first book in *The Ritchie and Fitz Sci-Fi Murder Mysteries.*

COMPLETE SERIES: THE TRAVELS OF SCOUT SHANNON

The complete six-book series *The Travels of Scout Shannon* begin with book one, *Under Falling Skies*.

Scout Shannon's whole family died the day the Space Farers dropped an asteroid on their domed city. Now she lives alone, out in the wild with only her dogs for company. She prefers it that way.

But Scout finds herself at a crossroads. One road leads back to a quiet life snug under the protective dome of a city. The other road leads to a life in the rebellion, a life of adventure and excitement but also danger. Dare she try to find the rebels hiding in the hills?

Then a chance encounter with a stranger from the other side of the galaxy threatens to derail what remains of Scout's life. The entire galaxy awaits her, if she survives the next four days.

Under Falling Skies, a young adult science fiction novel, set on a remote planet with a distinctly Old West feel. For fans of gunslinging women and young girl assassins. And dogs.

Under Falling Skies, the first book in *The Travels of Scout Shannon,* available everywhere now.

SCI-FI SERIAL PODCAST!

Check out my new monthly podcast of serialized science fiction: THE TALES OF THE CHAI MAKHANI TRIO!

Elyot loathes the massive Commonwealth ships that hover menacingly over his home world of Adghal. He hates the Commonwealth enforcers who harass the populace even more. But with his mother missing and presumed dead, Elyot keeps his head down and strives to avoid notice. And he succeeds until the day two strangers enter his life...

New episodes of this sci-fi serial drop every 1st of the month.

Now streaming on all major podcast platforms. Also available in eBook and print everywhere books or sold. For a complete episode listing, check out the page on my website.

ALSO FROM KATE MACLEOD

Love heists and capers? Then check out my new series, *The Vic Harper Capers*. The action starts with the novella THE THIRD POLE JOB.

Vic Harper and her gang retired wealthy from their life of thievery and heists. Whether in a luxury condo overlooking the river in Minneapolis or in a modernist mansion built into the side of a mountain in Colorado, life comes easy now.

Perhaps too easy.

When an old friend asks for a favor his niece, Vic and her mentor Chase Woodward leap at the chance to relieve a little of the boredom. But a quick bit of B&E in a wealthy suburb of Chicago leads to an even greater challenge.

The prize? Nothing much. Just the opportunity to level a playing field for their friend's niece.

But the heist? May prove to be their toughest ever. Because to get to the prize, they'll have to climb a mountain.

And not just any mountain. Their prize waits on the summit of Mount Everest.

THE THIRD POLE JOB, the first novella in *The Vic Harper Capers*. For those who love capers, heists and other impossible missions.

ALSO FROM RATATOSKR PRESS

Also from Ratatoskr Press, *The Witches Three Cozy Mystery Series* by Cate Martin, a mix of mystery and magic that begins with Book 1: *Charm School*.

Amanda Clarke thinks of herself as perfectly ordinary in every way. Just a small-town girl who serves breakfast all day in a little diner nestled next to the highway, nothing but dairy farms for miles around. She fits in there.

But then an old woman she never met dies, and Amanda was named in her will. Now Amanda packs a bag and heads to the big city, to Miss Zenobia Weekes' Charm School for Exceptional Young Ladies. And it's not in just any neighborhood. No, she finds herself on Summit Avenue in St. Paul, a street lined with gorgeous old houses, the former homes of lumber barons, railroad millionaires, even the writer F. Scott Fitzgerald. Why, Amanda can practically hear the jazz music still playing across the decades.

Scratch that. The music really, literally, still plays in the backyard of the charm school. Because the house stretches across time itself. Without a witch to protect this tear in the fabric of the world, anything can spill over. Like music.

Or like murder.

The complete series is out now, and it all starts with *Charm School*.

FREE EBOOK!

Like exclusive, free content?

To get two prequel short stories to THE RITCHIE AND FITZ SCI-FI MURDER MYSTERIES as well as a bonus prequel novelette to the completed six-book series THE TRAVELS OF SCOUT SHANNON, signup for my monthly newsletter at KateMacLeodWrites.com.

Thank you!

ABOUT THE AUTHOR

Photograph © 2016 Jonathan Conklin

Kate MacLeod has written stories which have appeared in *Analog*, *Strange Horizons* and *Mythic Delirium*, among other places. She is also the author of two young adult science fictions series: *The Travels of Scout Shannon*, and *The Ritchie and Fitz Sci-Fi Murder Mysteries*. She also contributes to a serialized science fiction podcast called *The Tales of the Chai Makhani Trio*. She currently lives in Minneapolis, Minnesota.

Find out more about the author and sign up for her newsletter at KateMacLeodWrites.com.

ALSO BY KATE MACLEOD

Novels

The Slums of the Solar System:

Mitwa

The Mars of Malcontents

The Whole World for Each

Books 1-3 Box Set

The Travels of Scout Shannon:

Under Falling Skies

In Quaking Hills

Among Treacherous Stars

Against Impassable Barriers

Over Freezing Altitudes

At Galactic Central

The Travels of Scout Shannon Books 1-3

The Travels of Scout Shannon Books 4-6

The Travels of Scout Shannon Books 1-6

The Ritchie and Fitz Sci-Fi Murder Mysteries:

Murder on the Intergalactic Railway

Murder in the Skies

Body in the Catacombs

Death on the Summit

An Undiplomatic Murder

A Lethal Betrayal

The Forgotten Planet

Raiding the Forgotten Derelict (Forthcoming September 2024)

Sci-Fi Novellas

The Intergenerational Tree

I Rise into a Daybreak

Caper Novellas

The Third Pole Job

The Twelve Days of Christmas Job

10-Story Collections

Tales of Blood and Ink

Tales of Old Gods and New

5-Story Collections

Tales from Heian-Kyo and Others

Tales from the Edges and Ends

Tales from Forgotten Days

Tales from Ancient and Future Times

Tales from Across Space

www.ingramcontent.com/pod-product-compliance
Lightning Source LLC
Chambersburg PA
CBHW050359190726
48284CB00007BB/2347